EARTHQUAKE
ALERT

Ben stopped brushing himself down and his head snapped sideways towards the forest.

A rustling sound swept through the trees below.

But that was impossible. There was no wind.

The ground began to shudder.

Several metres ahead, the grass and soil heaved up as if a giant mole was trying to break out into the air.

'What the hell is that?' Carly yelled. 'What's happening?'

Ben suddenly felt unsteady on his feet. 'I don't know!'

From under the ground, water welled upwards, loosening the earth around. The surface bubbled and churned like a pan of boiling soup. The solid ground all around them was turning into liquid mud.

Some other books by Jack Dillon

**SURVIVE! FIRESTORM
SURVIVE! HURRICANE HORROR**

SURVIVE!

EARTHQUAKE ALERT

Jack Dillon

PUFFIN BOOKS

For Adam
Special thanks to
Cherith Baldry and Ian Locke

PUFFIN BOOKS

Published by the Penguin Group
Penguin Books Ltd, 27 Wrights Lane, London W8 5TZ, England
Penguin Putnam Inc., 375 Hudson Street, New York, New York 10014, USA
Penguin Books Australia Ltd, Ringwood, Victoria, Australia
Penguin Books Canada Ltd, 10 Alcorn Avenue, Toronto, Ontario, Canada M4V 3B2
Penguin Books (NZ) Ltd, Private Bag 102902, NSMC, Auckland, New Zealand

On the worldwide web at: www.penguin.com

Penguin Books Ltd, Registered Offices: Harmondsworth, Middlesex, England

First published 1999
1 3 5 7 9 10 8 6 4 2

Text copyright © Working Partners Ltd, 1999
All rights reserved

Created by Working Partners Ltd, London W12 7QY

The moral right of the author has been asserted

Typeset in Bembo

Made and printed in England by Clays Ltd, St Ives plc

British Library Cataloguing in Publication Data
A CIP catalogue record for this book is available from the British Library

ISBN 0–140–38817–6

CHAPTER ONE

'I don't want to go to Venice,' Ben Fletcher muttered. 'You see one canal, you've seen 'em all.'

His mother, Marian, came in from the balcony of their holiday apartment, where she had been setting the table for supper.

'Venice is one of the great cities of the world,' she told him briskly. 'We'd be mad to come to Italy and not see it.'

'Huh,' said Ben.

He was sprawled in a deep armchair, long legs stretched out in front of him, sandy hair flopping into his eyes. He fiddled with the settings on his camera. It was new: a birthday present from his dad. Photography was his passion and interested him more than anything else.

'But Venice is beautiful.' His father, John Fletcher, came out of the kitchen, juggling plates of Parma ham and melon. 'You'll get some fantastic pictures there.'

'Not if we spend all day dragging round churches and art galleries.'

His father gave a long, elaborate sigh and disappeared on to the balcony with the plates. Ben's mum said, 'Look, Ben –'

'OK,' Ben interrupted her. 'I just don't want to go tomorrow, right? I've fixed up with Carly to climb the mountain and take pictures of the sun coming up.'

'Then you should have asked first.' Marian was starting to sound irritated. She hurried across the sitting room into the kitchen and reappeared with a handful of paper napkins. 'Ben, I wish you would help instead of just sitting there. We're never going to be ready in time. The Scotts will be here any minute!'

Ben put the camera aside, heaved himself to his feet and took the napkins from his mother. Ben's parents had invited the Scotts, the family from the apartment above, to join them for their evening meal.

Marian Fletcher had met Ann Scott while they were both having an early-morning swim. The Scotts came from the north of England, a long way away from the London-based Fletchers, and they visited Italy every year. They had three children: Tim, a university student, Carly, who was Ben's age, and baby Sara. Ben and Carly had become good friends in the few days they had known each other.

Out on the balcony, Ben folded the napkins into triangles and put one at each place. The sun was going down. The little Italian town, stretching down below the timeshare resort, was washed golden in the dying light. Ben could see the main square, the tower of the old church with its single bell, the formal gardens around the ruins of the medieval castle.

At the bottom of the hill a river looped around the edge of the town. The bridge was out of sight, but Ben knew it carried the main road south to Venice, about a hundred kilometres away. Sighing resignedly, he thought of himself stuck in the car and being carried along that road the following day.

If he leant out over the balcony, he could just see the mountain he wanted to climb instead. There was no snow on top, just pine forest straggling up its sides. Narrow paths criss-crossed the hill among the trees. Ben guessed there would be a terrific view from the top. Natural landscape interested him most of all.

He moved away from the rail and stuck his hands in his jeans' pockets as his mother came out with the rest of the plates of melon. 'Why can't we go to Venice another day?'

'Why can't you go with Carly another day?'

'Because the Scotts are going home at the weekend, and they've got stuff planned every other day.'

'Well so have we got stuff planned,' Marian said.

'Then you go to Venice and let me stay here.'

Ben went back into the sitting room, nearly colliding with his father and a bowl of Parmesan cheese. John wove a path round him and out on to the balcony. 'Don't think we're not tempted.'

'Oh, no,' his mother said. 'I'm not having

4

you hanging around here all day by yourself, or expecting Ann Scott to keep an eye on you when she has the baby to look after.'

Ben could feel frustration building up inside him. Trying to sound calm and reasonable, he said, 'OK then. Me and Carly will go up the mountain, see the sunrise, come straight back down again, and then we go to Venice. OK?'

'No,' John said, reappearing. 'Not OK. I know you, Ben Fletcher. Once we let you out of our sight, that's it. We'd be lucky to see you before lunchtime. I want to make an early start.'

All Ben's frustration spilled over. 'Dad, this is my holiday as well.' His voice was rising out of control. 'I don't have to do what you want all the time!'

The doorbell rang.

Marian hissed at him, 'Ben, please don't be so difficult!' She went to answer the bell.

Ben felt John's hand on his shoulder. 'We'll talk about this later,' his father said.

Then the door opened, and cheerful voices broke into the apartment. If the Scotts had heard Ben yelling, they gave no sign of it.

Tim led the way, long and lanky – and

vague, reminding Ben of a friendly stick insect. Graham Scott, just as tall and thin as his son, but nearly bald, lugged baby Sara's carrycot. Sara snuffled away inside. Ann Scott followed, giving Marian a peck on the cheek and thanking her for the invitation.

Carly came last of all. As soon as she saw Ben, she bounced across to him with a cheerful grin. Carly was always cheerful, and she always looked untidy. Her mass of dark hair was tangled, and she was wearing rumpled combat trousers and a khaki top.

'Hi!' she said. 'OK for tomorrow?'

Ben's mother was showing Graham where to leave Sara's carrycot in one of the bedrooms so she could sleep in peace. His father had taken Ann and Tim out on to the balcony. Out of their earshot, Ben muttered, 'No. I can't come. They want to go to Venice.'

'But it's our last chance!' Carly wailed.

Ben shrugged. 'What can I do?'

A spark of mischief lit Carly's face. Ben had seen that look before. She glanced from side to side, making sure no one could hear her, then murmured in Ben's ear, 'Let's go anyway.'

'I can't do that!'

'Why not? Look, Ben, we'll be leaving really early. Your mum and dad will be asleep.' Carly slapped him on the shoulder as they followed their parents outside. 'Come on, Ben. Let's go for it.'

Ben was still thinking about it as they took their places at the big round table on the balcony. By now it was growing dark. Lights were twinkling in the town below, and Marian had lit candles on the table. John opened a bottle of wine and filled everyone's glass.

Ben was starting to relax, his anger dying away. He almost wished Carly hadn't suggested going up the mountain without permission. He really didn't want the hassle there would be when he got back. But if he refused, Carly would think he was a wimp. He didn't know what to do.

He picked distractedly at his ham and melon. When he started to pay attention to the conversation around the table, Carly's dad was talking about the news in the local paper. Graham Scott taught Italian – one reason the Scotts always holidayed in Italy.

'There's a lot of talk about an earthquake,' he was saying.

7

'An earthquake?' Marian sounded alarmed. 'Are they expecting one?'

Graham Scott smiled. 'There's nothing to worry about. Italy gets its fair share of earthquakes. And so there's always talk.'

'Even so . . .' Ben's mum wasn't reassured.

'There hasn't been any activity around here for years,' Graham Scott explained. Ben could see why he was a teacher; he liked to tell you things, and in Ben's opinion he liked the sound of his own voice a bit too much. 'But they're always wondering when the next one will be. The article reported one of the locals saying the big one is on its way, but scientists at Milan University are talking about anything up to three or four years.'

'Oh, if that's all . . .' Marian said, relieved.

'Don't they know precisely?' Carly asked.

'No,' her dad said. 'It's very hard to predict an earthquake.'

Ann Scott took her last bite of melon, patted her lips with her napkin, and said, 'I thought they could predict everything these days.'

Ben was vaguely remembering what he'd done in Geography at school last year. It was something about the continents shifting.

'Don't the rocks move around, or

something?' he asked. 'Deep down inside the earth?'

Tim Scott came back from whatever planet he was currently occupying, smiled vaguely and said, 'The Japanese used to believe earthquakes were caused by a giant spider scuttling about underground.'

'Yuk!' said Carly, with a mock shudder.

'Well, I don't want to know, thanks very much,' Marian said. 'As long as there's not going to be one here, that's good enough for me.'

She started to collect the empty plates. Ann helped her, and they both went into the kitchen. John got up to fetch some more wine.

'You're right, Ben,' Graham Scott continued. 'The rocks do move. In this area, the stresses under the Adriatic Sea are pushing the rocks northwards. That's what forced the Alps up – over millions of years, obviously. You see –' he was well away by now – 'the earth is divided into about ten enormous sections called continental plates.'

Carly yawned ostentatiously and rolled her eyes. Ben tried to look politely attentive. After all, Graham Scott wasn't his dad.

With a sideways look at his daughter, Graham went on, 'The places where the plates meet each other are called faults. Like this. He laid a spoon and fork from his place setting side by side. 'America. Asia. OK?' Ben nodded. 'Stresses and strains build up in the rocks way below ground level, and sooner or later something has to give.' He slid the spoon and fork past each other. 'An earthquake.'

Carly inspected the spoon and fork with a puzzled frown and said, 'It looks . . . sort of small.'

Graham grinned and batted one hand at her; Ben was relieved to see he wasn't really annoyed.

'OK, lesson over. The point is – sorry.' He had to shift his fault line as Marian and Ann came back with big pots of pasta and sauce, followed by John with two bottles of cold wine misted from the fridge. 'The point is, scientists use seismographs to measure the earthquake when it happens, but there's nothing much to measure beforehand. That's why earthquake predictions aren't very accurate.'

Tim stopped shovelling pasta on to his

plate long enough to say, 'I read somewhere that you see strange lights in the sky before a big 'quake. And animals do weird things.'

'Pigs fly, you mean?' Carly stuck her tongue out at her brother.

Tim gave her a gentle smile and dolloped sauce on top of his pasta.

Ben wondered what it would be like if an earthquake struck. Just a mild one, that didn't do much damage. 'It might be interesting,' he said aloud.

'Interesting?' his mum said, raising her eyes. 'You'd find it really interesting, Ben, if the apartment block collapsed on top of you.'

'Squashed,' Tim said with relish. 'Like the meat in a sandwich.'

'Actually,' Graham Scott said, in teacher mode again, 'these days they know how to build so that the materials take the stress without –'

'Graham, we don't want to hear about all that.' Ann Scott interrupted before he could get into his stride. 'Why go on about something that isn't going to happen?'

Mr Scott looked annoyed for a moment, until Marian changed the subject by asking, 'Graham, tell us about Venice. We're going there tomorrow. What are the best things to see?'

Both the Scott parents started talking together, and then laughed. They would be well away for the rest of the meal, Ben thought. He didn't have much to contribute, and he was feeling uneasy again. Pretty soon he would have to make up his mind whether he was going with his mum and dad to Venice, or up the mountain with Carly.

While everyone was having coffee, Sara woke up and started wailing. Ann fetched her from the bedroom and gave her a drink of juice, but nothing seemed to settle her. Ann rocked her against her shoulder.

'She's not usually like this,' she said. 'Once she's off, she sleeps through till morning. I'm sorry, Marian, it would be tonight she decides to make a fuss. I'd better take her home.'

The moment came for Ben to make his decision. The Scotts were leaving. Everyone said their goodbyes quickly. Ann went out, jogging baby Sara as she turned to climb the stairs that led to the upstairs apartment. Graham followed with the carrycot and Tim drifted after him. Carly was left standing with Ben at the door.

'OK. I'm on for it,' he whispered. 'As soon as it starts to get light, give me a signal and I'll meet you by the main entrance.'

'Cool!' said Carly, her face beaming. Up above, Sara's howls reached a new crescendo. Ben could hear his mum behind him, clattering about in the kitchen. 'I'd better go,' Carly sighed. 'See you in the morning, then.'

'Sure thing. Let's get up with the larks and explore!'

CHAPTER TWO

Ben couldn't settle in bed that night. The air was hot and humid and he felt as if he was lying in a warm bath. Although he had left his window open, there was not a breath of wind, and the bedsheet stuck to him.

Sleep refused to come, partly because Ben was worrying about missing his dawn rendezvous with Carly and partly because, for some reason, every dog in the town seemed to be barking. Ben could hear them starting from quite close by, all the way down the hill and into the distance. One dog would bark and another would answer it, and then another. It seemed endless.

In the lulls between the spells of canine barking, Ben could sometimes hear the cries of baby Sara drifting down from the floor above.

He dozed uncomfortably, tossing and turning, reaching out to look at the luminous display on his watch, the seconds slowly counting down. Eventually he realized that it was time to make a move; it would soon be time to meet Carly. He went to the bathroom and then silently pulled on shorts and T-shirt and walking shoes, all the while listening for sounds of movement from his parents' room.

A low-pitched whistle from outside made him turn his head.

He slid into the sitting room. The balcony windows were locked, and Ben didn't want to make any noise opening them. He couldn't see Carly, but he heard her signal again. He picked up his camera bag, checked his wallet to make sure he had some lire for emergencies, then he found a piece of scrap paper and scribbled a note: 'Gone up the mountain. Back in time for Venice.' He propped the paper up against the kettle in the kitchen where his mum would be sure to find it when she got up. Then he let himself out of the apartment as quietly as he could.

Carly was sitting on a low stone wall by the path outside their apartment block. 'You made it!' she said. In the grey light coming from the east, Ben could see that she looked pleased to see him.

'Did you ever doubt me?' he joked.

'Have you got everything?' she asked.

Ben patted his camera bag. 'All equipment present and correct. You?'

Carly dipped into one of the side pockets of her trousers and pulled out a packet of chewing gum. She waved it at him and grinned. 'Only the essentials.'

Ben laughed and playfully tugged her to her to feet. 'Come on, let's get going.'

Without looking back, he led the way at a quick pace down the path, past the reception area of the resort and out through the main gates. They were on their way.

Soon they reached the first whitewashed houses of the little town, small buildings with bright flowers that climbed their courtyard walls and scented the gardens. At this hour, there was hardly anybody about and little traffic. The main road through the town led past the castle and the Orto del Castello with its neatly clipped shrubs lining the smooth lawns and pathways. Then the road wound through the Piazza Maggiore, where in the middle of the day there were market stalls and busy pavement cafés. Now everything was quiet. Even the dogs had stopped barking.

Beyond the town the road crossed the river via the Ponte Nuovo, an airy suspension bridge; its huge white struts vanished into a mist that clung to the water's surface. Ben paused in the middle and listened to the river chuckling over stones. It sounded eerie in the grey mist and silence.

Carly leant over the side and dropped a pebble into the fast-flowing river. 'Bet that's a bit chilly,' she muttered.

Ben tugged her arm. 'Later. We'll miss the sunrise.'

On the other side of the bridge, one of the roads narrowed and led off towards the mountain. As they climbed, they left the river mist behind them and Ben could see the morning light strengthening in the eastern sky. Luckily there was still no sign of the sun.

The road snaked back and forth across the hilly lower slopes of the mountain. Ben's camera bag bounced uncomfortably on his hip and a trickle of sweat ran down his back. He stopped briefly to catch his breath.

'Hey! You've been eating too many chips!' Carly said with a grin.

Ben shrugged off the jibe and looked back along the way they had come. He could see the river below, a section of road leading to the bridge where the mist had begun to clear, the town and, beyond that, the white blocks of the resort apartments where they were staying. He took his camera out. 'I'll take a picture of you for your mum,' he said. 'She'll like that.' He moved round in front of Carly and lined up the most stunning background he could find.

'Think your parents'll go easy on you when we get back?' Carly asked, grinning. 'Or are you in for the third degree?'

Ben winced as the camera clicked. 'Don't remind me.'

Through the viewfinder, Ben noticed that Carly's attention had been caught by something to his right near the side of the road.

'Hey!' she said. 'Look at this.'

Ben lowered the camera and strolled over

to her. She held out something on the palm of her hand: a tiny mouse, crouched and trembling.

'It's scared,' Ben said. 'Let it go.'

'I didn't catch him,' Carly said. 'He was like this when I saw him. I think he's forgotten the way home.' Gently she scratched the mouse's head. '*Ciao*, Topolino.'

'Topolino?'

'Mickey Mouse in Italian. Take his picture, Ben.'

Ben laughed. 'OK.'

He adjusted the lens for a close-up and photographed the tiny mouse perched on Carly's hand.

'He's sweet,' said Carly. 'I wish I could keep him.' She carefully set the mouse down in the grass and it scurried away. 'There you go, Mickey. Go home to Minnie. *Arriverderci*.' She straightened up, looking puzzled. 'I wonder what got into him. They don't usually sit like that out in the open.'

Ben put his camera away. 'Maybe something scared him.'

'When they're scared, they hide. Maybe he was ill. Didn't look it, though. Oh, well.' Carly shrugged. 'I guess we'll never know.'

They continued on. The crunching stones underfoot soon gave way to softer earth and old pine needles as the path grew steeper and led into a forest of evergreens. The pine trees were all around them, dark and straight, with a spicy, resinous smell. Carly stopped and sniffed appreciatively. 'This is great, isn't it? Smell Mother Nature!'

Ben grinned at her. 'I thought you were a party animal, Carly?'

'Nah, I'm an outdoor type, really.' She spread her arms dramatically. 'I love the trees, the hills, the sky –'

'The designer walking boots – ow!' Ben doubled over as Carly poked him in the stomach.

Laughing, she danced ahead of him up the path.

'I'll get you for that!' he threatened.

'Got to catch me first!'

He broke into a run, but almost at once slowed down again. The slope was too steep and the forest too solemn a place for playing games.

He sensed that Carly felt it too when she waited for him to catch up and walked on by his side.

Their footsteps made a crackling sound; everything else was quiet.

'You'd think there'd be birds,' said Carly.

Ben gazed around him, but saw nothing except for the silent ranks of trees. 'Maybe they're still asleep.'

'No, it's getting lighter. What about the dawn chorus?' She shivered and trudged on up the path.

Gradually the pine trees thinned out. On the edge of the forest, they passed a forester's small wooden hut. The door was closed and the windows were covered by opaque shutters. There was definitely nobody at home.

Ben too began to sense the eerie atmosphere that was affecting Carly. Without sharing their thoughts, they tramped upwards over thin grass, with rocks poking up here and there. Every now and then they saw a solitary tree, twisted by the wind. But there was still no sign of the sun.

'I don't think we're going to make it in time,' said Carly anxiously.

Ben grunted and increased his pace, his feet slipping on loose stones. 'Yes we will. It's not far now.' The close atmosphere was beginning to worry him. Somehow he was finding it hard to breathe, and not just because he was moving uphill rapidly. The air seemed heavy. It was as if everything around him was waiting for something to happen.

He stopped abruptly. 'Carly, do you remember what your brother said? About earthquakes? How animals know they're coming and they behave in weird ways.'

'Oh, come on –' Carly began as she drew level with him.

'No, listen. All the dogs were barking last night. And Sara was crying – maybe babies feel it the same as animals do.'

'Dogs bark. Sara's teething.' Carly set off up the slope again. 'Are we doing this or not?'

Ben scrambled to catch her up. 'And what about that mouse? And why aren't the birds singing?'

'How should I know? Look, Ben, you don't want to take any notice of Tim. He's into crop circles and ley-lines and all sorts of weird stuff. He says things just to wind us up. Ignore him.'

All of a sudden, Ben's chest was heaving. He could feel sweat trickling down his forehead, and inside his T-shirt. He turned to glance back the way they had come.

The forest was a dark mass below. Just on its edge he could see the mountain hut, still shuttered and silent. Beyond the forest, much further down, the river shone in the dawn light. He could just make out part of the town; the buildings were tiny at this distance. Everything was still; it was almost as if he was looking at one of his own photographs.

'Come on!' Carly yelled from up above on the rocky slope.

Ben began to climb again, trying to shake off his growing uneasiness. Carly had to be right. Earthquakes – really big earthquakes – didn't happen all that often. It was stupid to think that he would be caught in one, just because a few animals were acting strangely.

All the same, Ben wished he was somewhere else. Safely back now in the apartment perhaps – even if he had to face a row with his parents. Or on the road to Venice in a stuffy car. Anything would be better than being out on this mountain, alone except for Carly, and this menacing feeling gathering all around him. He tried to hurry, so that he could quickly take his pictures and head back.

Ahead of him, Carly had disappeared over

a shoulder of the mountain. Ben scrambled to catch her up; when she came into view, she had halted and was shading her eyes against the growing light, staring across the slope to her right.

A man was standing there.

As Ben caught sight of him, the figure cupped his hands to his mouth and shouted something. His voice was faint.

'What's he want?' he asked Carly.

Carly shook her head. 'Don't know. Can't hear him properly.'

The man had stopped trying to shout, and now was waving his arms in the air. Ben thought he looked worked up about something, and he seemed to be pointing down the mountainside, indicating they should climb down.

'Something's bugging him,' Ben said. 'Are we on private property?'

'Don't know. Anyway, we're not doing any harm. I'm not going back now.'

She started to climb again. At the same moment, the man gave up whatever he was trying to tell them and hurried away down the slope towards the town.

Ben watched him trudge out of sight. His

uneasiness returned. Had the man been angry? Or afraid? Was he telling them off, or was he trying to warn them?

While Ben had hesitated, lost in thought, Carly had almost reached the top. His camera bag had swung forward and was hanging awkwardly in front of him. Then he saw Carly. She had her back to him and she was looking down at something.

'Ben!' she called out. 'Come and look at this.'

Ben thought he detected a note of anxiety in her voice, but that was stupid. There was nothing to be scared of. He dragged himself up the last few metres of the slope, and stood beside her. 'Phew! At last. We made it. What are you looking –'

His voice trailed off.

In front of them the ground dropped away into a huge, cup-shaped hollow. The bottom of it was filled with water, a hidden mountain lake just short of the summit. Because the hills rose so steeply all around it, the lake itself was still in shadow.

All across the dark surface of the water, lights were moving. Waves rippled across the lake, causing sparks to dance gently in the air.

'What is it?' Carly's voice was soft, shaking a little.

'I don't know. Tim said . . . weird lights –' Ben's throat was suddenly very dry.

'You're not still thinking it's an earthquake!'

Carly had to be right. The ground was still solid under their feet. Maybe they were feeling scared over nothing. There must be a simple explanation.

Quickly Ben got out his camera, crouched down and snapped a couple of shots of the lake and the strange lights. No one would ever believe this unless they had photographic proof.

Then, as he was putting his camera away, the lake changed. The lights faded. The water began to move. It sloshed back and forth, up and down the surrounding slopes like tea slopping over the edge of a cup. Ben still could not feel any movement in the ground where they were standing.

Carly seemed to draw a long, painful breath, then she croaked, 'What on earth is going on?'

Ben gripped her arm. His voice wavered. 'I don't know – but let's get out of here.'

CHAPTER THREE

Ben pulled Carly away from the edge of the cavernous hollow, back down the slope they had just climbed. Carly didn't resist him.

The summit of the mountain rose to their left, and from behind the dark, humped shape the sun came up at last, too bright to look at. The mountain slopes came to life in the sunlight and for a few seconds everything looked so different that Ben was not sure which way they had come. Then he caught sight of the tiny gap in the trees where the path emerged, not far from the mountain hut.

'Let's go,' he said, beginning the climb

down. 'I don't think we should hang around this place.'

'I'm right behind you,' said Carly, alternately clinging on to his arm and the bag strap as they moved away from the edge.

At every moment Ben was expecting the ground to shake, or maybe even to swallow him up. He wanted to run, to get away, to be anywhere with other people instead of just the two of them on this deserted mountain.

As they slipped and scrambled down the steep slope, Ben heard a new sound that disturbed the unnatural stillness of the morning. It was a church bell, very faint, rising from the town below.

'Listen,' said Ben, jamming his feet against a boulder to check his descent.

Carly skidded into him and put her arms around him for balance. 'What is it?'

'Church bells. It's not Sunday.'

'So it's probably a festival. They have them all the time in Italy. Come on.'

Ben followed, but he wasn't entirely sure that her explanation made sense. Carly hadn't sounded sure, either. It was too early in the morning to be ringing a bell. And although he couldn't hear it clearly, he didn't think it sounded as if it was being rung properly.

He half tripped and half slid the rest of the way to the bottom of the steepest part of the slope. There the ground in front of him fell away more gently, a mixture of thin soil, sparse grass and stones. The dark line of the forest was a couple of hundred metres away. The irregular sound of the church bell could still be heard coming from the town far below.

Carly had stopped to wait for him. Her hands were on her hips and she was tapping one foot, exaggerating her impatience. Ben broke into a run, the heavy camera bag thudding against his side. He skidded to a halt and bumped shoulders with Carly.

'Steady,' she said. 'Break an ankle up here, and – Ben!'

Ben stopped brushing himself down and his head snapped sideways towards the forest.

A rustling sound swept through the trees below.

But that was impossible. There was no wind.

The ground began to shudder.

Several metres ahead, the grass and soil heaved up as if a giant mole was trying to break out into the air.

'What the hell is that?' Carly yelled. 'What's happening?'

Ben suddenly felt unsteady on his feet. 'I don't know!'

From under the ground, water welled upwards, loosening the earth around. The surface bubbled and churned like a pan of boiling soup. The solid ground all around them was turning into liquid mud.

Ben couldn't decide whether to run or stay where he was.

Carly's grip on his arm tightened. Her fingernails were digging instinctively into his skin.

They were both open-mouthed, struggling to speak, unable to make any sound other than a rising 'Aaaaargh!'

The ground in front of them erupted.

A jet of mud shot into the air and bubbled and gushed like a fountain. Mud and pebbles rained down.

Ben tried to protect his face with one arm as Carly huddled against him to save herself.

Ben looked up. 'Run! Back to the rocks!' he cried.

Mud spattered across his face and into his eyes, momentarily blinding him. He wiped a hand across his face, blinking to clear his vision. He tasted mud in his mouth and the smell of wet earth filled his nostrils.

Carly screamed.

The ground lurched under his feet. He began to sink.

He was trapped on the area of ground that had turned to liquid.

Carly's grip on him loosened as she moved away.

He nearly overbalanced as his camera bag swung forward. Staggering, he took a few more paces into what had been a mountain slope and which now felt like a swamp. Mud oozed over his ankles.

Carly's screaming was high-pitched and piercing over the dull roar of the moving earth.

Desperately, Ben wiped his sleeve over his eyes. The fountain had died down but the earth under his feet was flowing downwards, following the gravity of the slope and taking him with it.

A few metres away now, Carly struggled. She had slipped sideways, engulfed in mud; all Ben could see was her head and a shoulder and one wildly waving arm.

'Ben!' she yelled. 'Help me!'

Ben tried to reach her, floundering across the slope. He was terrified of falling. If he did, they would both be swallowed up. But all the while he was sinking deeper himself. The mud was up to his knees now, clinging round him with a horrible squelching noise as he tried to wade through it. He glanced back, but the more solid rock was far behind them now, and every second was taking them further from it.

Carly's screams had sunk to frightened, gasping cries. She was sinking lower and finding it hard to hold her head up.

'Hang on!' he cried. 'I'm coming!'

All the time they were both moving relentlessly downwards as the mud and earth channelled through a valley-like spout in the ground towards the forest.

Ben summoned all his strength to plough through the mud, but by now firm ground was a distant memory; his feet kicked underneath him but found no resistance. He didn't know what he could do to help Carly even if he reached her. And at the back of his mind was a more frightening thought: the earth turned liquid in just a few seconds.

What if it went solid again? Would they be buried?

The mud was almost up to his waist by now. It had engulfed his camera bag, and its weight was dragging him down further. He started to pull the strap off his shoulder to free it, thoughts of how furious his dad would be if he lost his new camera instantly discarded. As he let it go, he saw something ahead that made him lift his muddy arm and point.

'Carly! Look!'

Just a few metres beyond where Carly was struggling, Ben saw the mountain hut. Incredibly, it had been dislodged by the landslide and had moved several metres. It was tilted over, half buried, and was slowly sliding down with the rest of the earth and grass and stones on the slower-moving edges of the river of mud. It looked like a capsized boat lost at sea in a storm.

'Carly!' Ben yelled. 'Can you get to it?'

At first he thought Carly hadn't understood. He could see her terrified face streaked with mud. Her hair was matted. Her hands pawed at the surface as if she was trying to swim.

Ben yelled her name again, gesturing

towards the hut. Carly looked over her shoulder. At least now she could see what he meant, and she began wallowing through the swamp towards it. Ben blew out his breath in relief. She had guts. There was a chance. Now all he had to do was reach the hut himself.

He found he could make some progress by kicking and paddling with his hands. He tried not to think how fast he was sinking, how quickly he was moving away from the hut. He glanced to one side and saw that he was being carried down towards the line of trees. They looked uneven, like dominoes that had been knocked over, and he realized that some of them too must have been caught in the landslide. They were close now, and they were solid – something to hold on to until they found a way out. If there was one.

Still concentrating on staying afloat, he was up to his armpits now. He let the mud flow take him. In any case he was too exhausted to do much more. He realized it could only have been a few minutes since the ground had given way, but he felt as if he had lived through several hours of panic and struggling.

He turned his head, meaning to shout something encouraging to Carly. Renewed terror gripped him, almost like the panic he had felt when he imagined the ground growing solid again.

He could see the surface of the flowing mud, and debris carried along with it.

He could see the mountain hut, part of its roof and one corner still sticking into the air.

But he couldn't see Carly.

'Carly!' he yelled. 'Carly! Where are you?'

There was no answer.

CHAPTER FOUR

Ben went on shouting Carly's name until the mud flow slammed him against the first of the half-submerged uprooted trees at the edge of the forest. The breath was knocked out of him.

Desperately he grabbed hold of one of the thick dry branches above the flow and hauled himself upwards. The mud resisted, but he increased his efforts and with a long sucking noise he gradually came free and was able to lie flat along an exposed section of the trunk.

Almost immediately he noticed the torrent of mud slowing down, settling, lessening in its immense destructive force.

His tree had collapsed against several others – all held in place by those that were still standing. Ben reasoned that the ground must still be solid in what remained of the forest.

His body felt like one huge bruise. Part of him wanted to get up, reach firm ground again and run. Another part just wanted to lie there and forget everything. But he knew the one thing he must do: go and look for Carly.

He lifted his head and looked around. Further along the line of trees, the mountain hut had come to rest. It was tilted over with one corner of the roof poking upwards; Ben could see a side wall and part of a window; the rest had disappeared under the surface of the mud and was probably halfway down the mountain by now. Cautiously, on hands and knees, holding on to the branches of the flattened trees beneath him and ignoring the way they shifted under his weight, Ben began to make his way towards it.

He tried calling Carly's name again. He had to find her. She must be close by. Ben didn't want to think about her being already far away, buried under tonnes of viscous mud.

He had nearly reached the hut when he

heard a scrabbling sound coming from the other side. A dark, mud-encrusted shape appeared and flopped across the lowest part of the roof.

'Carly!' Ben exclaimed in relief.

Carly didn't answer. She snaked forward on to the mat of fallen trees and branches. She was caked in mud from head to foot. Her hair, hands, clothes, face and body were all covered. Two bright white eyes shone out from her face and almost made Ben want to laugh at how ridiculous she looked.

Nevertheless, she was alive.

Ben crawled towards her as she lay, coughing and retching, vomiting up the mud she had swallowed.

'Carly?' he said nervously. 'Carly, are you OK?' He reached out and touched her shoulder.

His hand flew back as she convulsed and spat more mud out of her mouth.

Carly looked at him for a long moment before she spoke, gasping with the effort of forming words. 'No – I'm not OK. Nobody but you . . . would ask that. Get me off here, will you?'

Ben lifted himself up, held his friend

tightly round the waist and half carried, half dragged her across the fallen trees to the solid ground among the trees beyond. When they reached it, she collapsed again and crouched in a tight bundle, shaking. It should be possible to get home, Ben thought, if only Carly could move. He felt far too exhausted even to think about carrying her all the way back to the resort.

Not sure what to do, Ben knelt beside her and waited.

Looking back up the slope, he could see that the mud slide had almost stopped. A huge gash had been torn in the side of the mountain and he couldn't tell where the path on which they started had been; it was no longer there. He guessed that it had been somewhere near the slowest-moving edge because if it had been any further to their right, both of them would have been carried away by the fastest part of the flowing mud. Probably to their sticky deaths.

Down the slope, the liquid earth had carved its way past the forest edges and carried rocks and debris for several hundred metres.

'Carly?' he tried again several minutes later.

SURVIVE! EARTHQUAKE ALERT

Carly looked up at him. She started laughing, though the laughter had a hysterical edge to it. 'What wouldn't I give for a hot shower!' She slicked her hair back with both hands; mud oozed between her fingers. 'I thought I'd had it, for sure.'

'Can you walk?' Ben asked tentatively.

'Got to.' She held out her hand and Ben hauled her to her feet. She leant on him for a minute and then started trudging determinedly downwards.

Ben walked at her side. He was thinking about the long journey back down the mountain and then along the road and through the town.

'Maybe we could hitch a lift,' he suggested.

Carly laughed again. 'Would you let us in your nice clean car?'

Ben thought not. He was nearly as filthy as Carly. His T-shirt and shorts were glued to his body. He could feel grime squishing between his toes and wedged beneath his fingernails. Nobody who saw them would want to stop for them. And what were their parents going to say? There would be the row to end all rows! On the other hand, he thought, not everybody has an excuse like ours. Not everybody gets caught in a landslide at dawn on a lonely Italian mountain.

He realized that he was so tired his mind wasn't working properly. It was stupid to worry about the trouble they would be in at home. They had enough trouble where they were. He couldn't even be sure that the landslide was over.

He wanted to run, to get out of the danger zone as quickly as he could, but he could only just about force one foot in front of the other to keep moving. Carly certainly couldn't go any faster. She was exhausted. They needed to rest, but this wasn't the right place or the right time.

Hours seemed to pass before they emerged from the cover of the trees.

When Ben eventually looked up at the sun, he could see it was still early morning. He felt he had lived a whole lifetime since the sun came up. He glanced at his wrist where his watch should have been, but he hadn't even noticed that it had already gone. Lost in a sea of mud.

'Must be nearly breakfast time,' he said. 'We'll soon be down now.'

Carly's shoulders were slumped and she

looked at her feet as she and Ben went on tramping down the slope. Ben thought she might give up at any minute, but he urged her to keep going, telling her he could see the path again.

Soon they rejoined the narrow path on the lower slope of the mountain near the place where Ben had taken his first picture of the day and Carly had found the mouse. Ben stood in the same spot as earlier and remembered how peaceful everything had looked.

Now he couldn't believe his eyes.

The suspension bridge had collapsed. The elegant white struts lay in a jumble on either bank and in the surging midst of the river itself. The stone piers had crumbled and choked the water flow with their massive bulk. River water was creeping over the land on either side as the main channel lay blocked. On both banks, the roads leading to the bridge were clogged with queues of cars. Even at this distance, Ben could hear the faint sound of horns.

'No!' Ben said explosively. 'I don't believe it!'

'It *was* an earthquake,' Carly said, her voice

limp with disbelief. She sat down in the dirt with a cloud of dust. 'It wasn't just in the mountains. They had it here too.'

Ben dropped to his knees and then lay down. 'This is not happening.'

He propped himself up on one elbow and looked out across the town. He could make out the blur of movement in the streets; the buildings themselves looked more or less undamaged.

The white apartment blocks of the resort were still standing.

Maybe it wasn't so bad after all. Maybe the earthquake had stopped at the river, Ben thought, or maybe it hadn't been strong enough to destroy buildings.

Down by the river, the flood waters were spreading. The main part of the town was built up the side of the hill, and Ben didn't think the water would rise high enough to threaten it. However, every minute that went by would make it harder to cross. He knew they shouldn't be sitting here; they would have to go on.

Carly looked as if she was asleep. He shook her gently.

She stirred, muttering, 'Whassat? Go away.'

Her arm flailed at him, but she sat up, blinking, and let Ben pull her to her feet.

'We have to get back,' he said.

'OK.' Carly coughed and slapped at herself to shake off some of the mud. She tugged her clingy shirt away from her chest. It was torn, and her arms were scratched and crusted with dried blood.

It began to dawn on Ben what a narrow escape she must have had and he admired her resilience even more now.

'Let's go,' she said determinedly.

They joined the main road not far from the bridge. As they approached it, the sound of noisy horns grew much louder, and they could see queues of dusty cars on both sides. A few of the drivers had got out on to the road and were standing arguing with one another – all punctuated with a lot of arm-waving and colourful language. A policeman with a walkie-talkie was moving along the queue as Ben watched. He guessed the man was trying to reassure everybody.

'Better stay clear of that lot,' Ben said. 'No one's going to help us get over there. They'll just hold us up.' Ben's growing sense of worry about his parents' state of mind spurred him on. They must know he was missing, and he shuddered to think what conclusions they had already jumped to about his safety.

Ben and Carly turned off the road and scrambled down a slope covered with tussocks of grass and sweet-smelling herbs. After about a hundred metres the ground levelled out and disappeared into the flood water.

Carly halted. 'Any ideas?'

Ben stood beside her and looked across the river – which was now a slowly spreading lake. Not far downstream were the twisted ruins of the bridge. Though most of the channel was choked with stones and girders, there were gaps where the water moved through fiercely. It wouldn't be possible to climb across the wreckage, even if no one stopped them.

'The water might not be too deep,' he said. 'The river's pretty shallow – you could wade across it.'

'You could once,' Carly retorted. 'If you're thinking of wading across that now, you're out of your tiny mind, Ben Fletcher. We've just had an earthquake, remember? There could be bottomless pits in there that we know nothing about.'

'But we've got to get across!' Ben protested. 'We don't know what might be happening in the resort.'

Carly shrugged. 'I know, but I'm sorry, Ben. I've had my swim for this morning. There's no point risking our lives if we don't have to.'

For a moment Ben wondered whether to leave her and try to swim across the lake by himself – she was safe enough now. He was a strong swimmer; the distance would be no problem, and probably he could wade part of the way. But he was very tired, and he had to admit that Carly was right: he had no idea what hidden deeps or currents there might be.

'Let's try upstream,' he suggested.

Carly fell in behind him with no argument as he set off along the riverbank. The sound of car horns and angry voices died away behind them. Ben noticed again how quiet it was. Still no birds. Another fear was added to his worries about his parents. Was it over? Or did the birds know that there was still more to come? He'd heard about the threat of aftershocks when an earthquake strikes. Perhaps if he didn't think about it, he could pretend that they weren't still in danger.

As they made their way upstream the flooding wasn't so bad, though the river was still lapping above its banks. Part of the bank had given way in places and had slid down into the river; they had to wade through the shallows and it became harder to keep their footing and make progress.

Soon the banks began to rise into a kind of gorge, with the river flowing along the bottom. If the channel became really narrow, the water would be higher and faster, harder still to cross.

Eventually their way was blocked by a spit of land jutting out into the river. With the water lapping against his ankles, Ben edged round it, grabbing at clumps of grass and projecting roots to keep his balance.

On the other side, rocks rose up out of the water. Debris from the landslide had already piled up against them, and the river was bringing still more down from the hills. As he waited for Carly to catch up to him, Ben examined the obstacle in their path. It was fairly solid; a couple of uprooted pines were caught in it, and it seemed to stretch right across the river.

'We could try here,' he suggested to Carly as she joined him.

Carly splashed through the shallow water at the river's edge as far as the rocky outcrop. Warily she climbed out on to the collected debris. It shifted a little under her weight, but it held.

'Seems OK,' she said. She looked back at Ben, flashing him a cheerful grin. 'Let's go for it. You wait here till I'm across. It might not hold both of us.'

Ben had intended to try it out first himself, but Carly was already clambering across the tangle of trunks and branches. About halfway across, she scrambled crablike on to a flat rock, turned back and waved. 'Fish me out if I fall in!' she yelled.

'At least you'll get a bath!' Ben yelled back.

Carly gave him the thumbs-up and moved on. Her progress grew slower; it looked as if the mass of debris was not so stable at the far side of the river. Ben watched agonizingly as it swayed beneath her; but it held, and she reached another rock close to the far bank. She had to jump the rest of the way, and she landed on hands and knees in the mud at the edge of the water.

She stood up and shook her dripping hands at Ben with a look of disgust. 'Nothing to it! Come on!'

Cautiously Ben ventured out on to the first rock and tentatively put all his weight on a trunk that looked more solid than the rest. Edging along on hands and knees, he felt the earth lurch as he moved and he heard the water gurgling underneath.

'I'll never bunk off again,' he muttered through his teeth. 'Promise.'

The first tree trunk crossed another that led him as far as the flat rock where Carly had stopped and waved. Ben stopped there as well, to rest; he was shaking with the strain of expecting everything to give way at any moment. He let out a long sigh of relief to have something solid under him again.

'Get on with it!' Carly yelled from the far bank. 'You going to stay there all day?'

Taking a deep breath, Ben went on. There were no large trees in the next section, just branches and roots and underbrush which rocked under him like a hammock. He wanted to give up, but he made himself keep going, eyes fixed ahead to where he was putting his hands and knees.

'You can swim if you have to,' he said to himself.

Then he heard Carly yelling. He looked up. She was jumping up and down on the bank, waving frantically at something upstream.

A roar drowned her voice. Ben turned his head to see a wall of water gushing down the gorge. It was brown with mud and topped with filthy foam, like thousands upon thousands of litres of cappuccino coffee. Tree trunks were bobbing around in it like matchsticks. Ben flung up an arm as it smashed into him. The mat of debris underneath him tore free. Ben's cries were drowned by a mouthful of water as he broke through the flimsy mesh and was plunged into the turbulent river.

CHAPTER FIVE

After several desperate seconds with his head under the water and his lungs exploding, Ben resurfaced, gasping and spluttering for air. Brown water surged all around him. He had lost all sense of direction, and for the moment he could not see either bank of the river. He kicked out at random, collided with something hard, and went under again.

The fierce current rolled him over and over. He was not sure which way was up. Just as he felt he could hold his breath no longer, his head broke surface. He trod water, desperately trying to get his bearings.

The river was littered with floating debris. A couple of metres away, a whole tree was being swept along; Ben struck out for it, thrashed his way through the flimsy outer branches and managed to pull himself up on the main trunk to see where he was.

The river was carrying him back downstream towards the ruined bridge. The thought of being dashed against one of the crumbled piles filled him with terror. He had to get out – and quickly.

The far bank he had been aiming for was not too far away. Carly was running along at the water's edge, keeping pace with him. 'Ben!' she yelled.

He raised a dripping arm to show he had seen her. He glanced downstream; the bridge was in sight, but still distant. Now or never, Ben thought. He let go of the tree trunk and swam vigorously across the current.

For a couple of horrible minutes he thought he wasn't going to make it. He summoned all his reserves of strength to combat the power of the raging water, and at last he was splashing in the shallows, close to the bank.

Carly knelt on the edge, stretching out a hand. Ben reached down and his feet found the bottom. Breathing hard, he squelched on to dry land and fell to his knees.

Carly crouched beside him. 'Ben, are you OK?'

Gradually, Ben got his breath back. 'Still alive. No bits missing. Wet.' He staggered to his feet, knowing that if he prolonged it any longer he would never get up.

Now it was Carly's turn to help him, and together they sloshed away from the riverbank. 'Come on, partner. Not long to go now.'

At last, they were upstream of the bridge and only a few hundred metres from the first, outlying buildings of the town. They needed to get around these to reach their apartment building.

At the bridge, police and drivers were working together to divert the traffic away from the advancing flood water. As Ben and Carly drew closer, they could see two cars caught up in the wreckage of the bridge itself, their twisted metal gleaming in the sun, water surging through their shattered windows. They must have been crossing the bridge at the moment it collapsed; Ben hoped the drivers had got out safely.

Before they reached the bridge, they came

to a lane that led off more directly towards the town, and they turned into it.

Ben was thinking about the hot shower and the huge breakfast he would have when they got back to their building, when Carly stopped abruptly. She had sensed movement up ahead.

She pulled at Ben's arm. 'Ben – what's that?' Something small and brown was scuttling across the grass, running towards them from the direction of the town. It moved in a series of short rushes. As it drew closer, Carly exclaimed, 'Ugh! It's a rat!'

Ben had never been this close to a rat before. He recognized the arched body, the wedge-shaped head, the coarse brown fur and stringy tail. It scurried past them only a metre or so away, just as Carly said, 'Ben, there's another.'

'And another!' exclaimed Ben.

A stream of rats were leaving the town and heading towards the river. *Rats leaving a sinking ship,* Ben thought. Did the rats know that something was going to happen, just as the birds and the mice had known earlier? He shook his head. Surely not. But then, who knew what Italian rats got up to?

Scanning the ground carefully as they

walked, Ben and Carly set off again towards the town.

The lane soon joined a narrow road which led between various buildings: flimsy, whitewashed structures – storage sheds or workshops, Ben guessed. That was where the rats had come from.

Looking around, Ben detected something wrong with the light. Or perhaps it was his eyes. Everything was hard-edged. The sheds looked like something painted on a stage backcloth, not real at all.

He turned to Carly. 'I don't like –' he started to say but didn't have a chance to finish his sentence.

All around them, a roaring sound began to increase in volume. It sounded like an express train, distant at first, but coming rapidly closer. Unlike a train, however, it wasn't coming from any one direction. It was everywhere: in the air, in the ground, tingling in the drums of their ears.

Seconds after the sound had begun, the ground shook.

'Beeeeeeen!' Carly's voice wavered as it escaped from her mouth.

Ben grabbed at Carly to keep his balance,

and they stood clinging together, petrified. Over the roaring noise, the church bells started up again. Screams rang out from the direction of the town but, as the roaring grew, it drowned them out. In front of their eyes the nearest building folded and collapsed in a cloud of dust.

Ben wanted to run, but he didn't know where to. Not into the town, where they could be crushed by falling stones. Not back to the flooded river and the broken bridge. There was nowhere to go.

This is it, he thought. This must be the real earthquake. The other one was just a warning.

The air above the ground was distorted, as if heat waves were rising up from it. A crack opened in the surface of the road, a gash showing raw soil. A strangled sound rose in Ben's throat. Was the ground going to swallow them up? As he stood, transfixed, a huge boulder came into view, rising as if it was light enough to float, while soil churned round it. Smaller stones leapt into the air, fell and bounced. One of them sprang sideways and struck Ben on the arm.

Ben was terrified that the ground was going to liquefy again and leave them floundering in mud, this time with no sanctuary close enough to reach. They were dangerously exposed. But the earth stayed solid despite its terrible shaking. The road they were standing on twisted as if it had broken free of its foundations and had come to life like some gigantic snake.

Ben and Carly staggered, still clinging to each other. Carly was yelling something into Ben's ear but, between panic and the rumbling that filled the air around them, Ben could not decipher her words.

The noise grew louder and louder. So loud, Ben thought his eardrums would burst. The medieval town wall stood firm, but beyond it, above the rooftops, Ben could see the bell in the church tower swinging back and forth. The sound of the bell was also drowned by the roaring of the earthquake. Then the tower started to tremble; for a moment it seemed to hang as if it was floating free of the earth before it fell slowly into ruin. Dust billowed up into the air, but the thunder of the earthquake was so loud Ben could not hear the falling stone or the final crashing of the bell.

The ground began to rise and fall like a roller coaster. As the waves reached Ben and Carly, they both lost their footing and fell. Ben lost his grip on Carly and was rolled over and over. Dust stung his eyes and clogged his mouth. He flailed about as he tried to find something solid to grab hold of. The ground heaved him up and then dropped away beneath him; he tried to stand up, but the shuddering earth flung him down again. Finally, he lay face down, trying to dig his fingers into the ground to stop himself being tossed around. A hand fastened around his wrist. He peered through the swirling dust to see Carly. The ground continued to shake crazily beneath them.

Ben didn't know how long they lay there, waiting for the end to come. He didn't know how he expected it to end. It seemed impossible that the noise would ever die away, that the earth would lie quiet again. Instead, he thought it was going to gape open and swallow them up. Maybe their families would never know what had become of them.

At last the rumbling died down.

The violent shaking of the ground subsided to a faint quivering. The air began to clear. Ben found it easier to breathe. He sat up, wiping his face and blinking dust out of his stinging eyes.

The town was still a whirlwind of dust and

Ben could hear screaming. People were running around in panic.

Beside him, Carly sat up and coughed. When she had caught her breath, she waved an arm towards the hill on the other side of the town.

'Resort . . . still there.'

Ben stared. Incredibly, the white apartment blocks were still standing. Almost as if in a dream, he heard Graham Scott telling them about how modern buildings could survive the stress of earthquakes.

But then, as he watched, the noise of the 'quake still echoing in his ears, a crack ran from the base to the top of one of the blocks; it looked like a clean black line drawn by a pencil. Gradually it widened until one side of the building slowly peeled away and cascaded downwards like a white waterfall. Balconies and awnings, chairs and tables plunged to the ground with the crumbling masonry, leaving a raw gash down the side of the block that still stood. A cloud of dust swelled and rose out of the wreckage.

Carly grabbed Ben's arm and shook him. 'Ben, that's our building! Our families could still be in there!'

CHAPTER SIX

Ben stared at the devastation. His vision still blurred, he wiped ineffectively at his eyes, in an attempt to wipe away what he had just seen. The white towers of the resort looked a long way away, as if they hadn't very much to do with the ruined town below.

Carly shook Ben again. 'We've got to do something!'

Ben coughed and spat out dust. 'We need to get up there.'

Carly let his arm go and staggered to her feet. 'Whatever's happened, even if –' She broke off, concentrating on trying to hide from Ben what she was really feeling. 'We have to find out.'

Ben forced himself to his feet and stood beside Carly. His legs felt shaky, almost as if the ground was still quivering.

'OK,' he said. 'Which way?'

Ahead of them, almost all the ramshackle buildings that had lined this back road into the town were completely flattened. Concrete blocks and corrugated iron were scattered over the road. Beyond them the town's medieval wall obscured their view and made it hard to see how much of the town had survived. Ben could see some rooftops through the haze of dust, and from somewhere on the far side a plume of smoke began to rise.

'We'll have to go round,' Carly said.

Ben shook his head. 'It'll take forever.'

Although the town was small, picking their way around the edges would take a lot longer than cutting through the middle. And there might be obstacles or fissures in the ground that they could not see from here. At least they had some idea of what the hazards might be in the town.

'Maybe you're right,' Carly said.

Ben started weaving his way through the jumble of stone and roofing panels. Carly followed, putting her feet down carefully. The ground was solid again, but Ben wondered whether he would ever be quite able to trust it again, whether he would be able to stop expecting it to give way under his feet.

An archway in the medieval wall led into the older part of the town. The wall itself, over a metre thick, seemed undamaged. Beyond it, broken glass from shop fronts littered the road; shop awnings had fallen and were draped over parked cars. Other cars had slewed across the road as if their drivers had been at the wheel when the earthquake struck; one or two had tipped over. Car alarms were blaring and there was the reek of petrol in the air.

People were milling about, some of them trembling with shock, others shouting instructions as if they were trying to restore some kind of order. One man was wandering along with a vacant look on his face, singing loudly and out of tune.

As Ben and Carly ventured through the archway and up the street, they were jostled by the crowd. A woman clutched at Ben, spun him round and peered into his face, then thrust him away, realizing he was not the person she was looking for.

Ben grabbed Carly's arm. 'Best not get separated.'

Carly nodded. 'If we do, head for the resort.'

It was hard to make their way through the press of people, avoiding the smashed cars and other wreckage. About halfway up the street, a tangle of power lines sagged from one side to the other, sparking fiercely where they came into contact with a metal shop sign. Ben felt uncomfortable as he ducked underneath, hugging the far wall away from the sparks.

Not much further up the street, they came to a crossroads where cars were backed up in all directions, blocking the road, slammed into walls or into each other. From one of them, down to the left, black smoke surged upwards. There was a strong smell of burning.

Beyond the crossing there was further damage to the buildings. The front of one shop had torn free and fallen flat into the road; the rest of it was undamaged and Ben could see tins and packets still on shelves on the back wall. A man with a broom, presumably the owner, was sweeping out the shop area almost as if it was business as usual.

'Is he going to sweep up the whole street?' Carly muttered.

Further along, the street led into the Piazza Maggiore, where there were fewer people than in the shopping area. The chairs and tables of the pavement cafés, with their striped umbrellas, had been thrown up against the walls like wreckage from a high tide. The brightly painted wooden band-stand in the centre of the square had survived. Ben thought it looked very odd. He half expected the uniformed bandsmen with their shiny instruments to come out and start playing, as he had heard them a few days before.

They crossed the square and entered the street at the far side. High walls threw it into deep shadow. Smoke and dust that had risen into the air covered the sun. Ben, still wet from the river, found himself shivering. Even so, he was beginning to feel more hopeful. They were making good progress through the town. The damage wasn't as bad as he had expected. Plenty of people were active and seemed to be uninjured. Probably his family and Carly's would be OK too. He had to keep on believing that.

Then they turned a corner and came in sight of the church. The Piazza di San Francesco was old and covered in cobbles.

The statue of St Francis of Assisi was no longer standing.

The whole square was now covered by chunks of the collapsed bell tower. In the centre, where the statue had stood, the bell had fallen. Made of bronze, it was taller than Ben in height, and it lay, tilted over. Part of the rim had bitten through the cobbles; the force of its fall had driven the bell part-way into the ground. Somewhere underneath it must be the statue of the saint, now no more than tiny fragments of its former self.

The rest of the church was still standing. On the steps, on the opposite side of the bell from Ben and Carly, a man in a black cassock gazed out over the square, the church priest. He was not moving or doing anything, he was just staring.

Ben shivered and this time it wasn't from the cold.

'That's really awful,' said Carly.

Ben nodded. The holy man's demeanour

summed up all the loss and the despair of the disaster.

Silently they moved on, skirting the bell and making their way up the next street that would lead them back to the resort. Here water was running down the gutter and spilling over the road from a broken pipe. Some small children were splashing around in it, while the house behind them had collapsed and their parents were poking about in the wreckage trying to salvage some of their belongings. Ben felt mean, hurrying past without offering to help, but he knew that they had to get back and find out what had happened to their own families first.

A little further on, the street was blocked by the ruins of yet another house. An old woman in black was sitting on the remains of one wall, weeping quietly, while a younger woman tried to comfort her. Ben and Carly turned back. Ben wondered how many more people he would see who had survived the earthquake but had lost almost everything they possessed. The town must be full of them.

They tried following a narrow alley that led more or less in the direction they wanted to go.

Not far along, Ben smelt smoke and, as the alley twisted, he glimpsed it billowing out of a house a few metres ahead. He could hear someone crying out and other voices replying, but at first he couldn't see anyone.

Then, as they drew closer, he made out dark figures darting to and fro amidst the smoke. Flames were spouting out of an upper window. Why fire, Ben wondered, on top of everything else? An electrical fault? An overturned cooker, or a gas leak?

Two men were throwing themselves at a closed wooden door, trying to break through it. Each time it gave a little more under their weight, but it did not open. Ben thought it looked as if the earthquake had squeezed it out of shape and jammed it in its frame.

'Someone must be inside,' Carly said hoarsely.

Ben wiped his streaming eyes. Both men were bigger and heavier than he was, but he instinctively moved forward and wriggled into the space beside them and thrust his shoulder against the door. With his additional weight, it burst open, and both men dived through it into the house.

Almost immediately a cat shot out between

Ben's ankles and hared off up the street; Carly gave way to giggles as Ben staggered and barely kept his balance. The men then reappeared with a woman who was carrying a baby, with a small boy hanging on to her hand. All of them stood and watched the house as flames devoured it.

Ben and Carly turned away; there was nothing more they could do.

The fire drove them round a corner into a maze of narrow alleys, some of them partly or completely blocked by fallen stone. They were not sure any longer of the right direction, but they tried to choose a way that would take them up the hill.

Eventually they came to a place where houses on both sides of the narrow street had fallen and filled the roadway with wreckage. A few people were stumbling over the heaps. Close to Ben, two men were trying to lift a heavy slab; as they shifted it to one side, Ben saw a hand sticking out from underneath as if it was reaching up for help.

He grabbed Carly and spun her round. 'Come on. We'll have to go back.'

Carly had gone white, and Ben realized that she had seen the frozen hand too.

Through her teeth she said, 'What's the use? We can't help. What good are we?' She sounded furious.

She pulled away from Ben's hand, striding back the way they had come.

Ben swallowed his sudden feeling of sickness and followed her.

They cut through another alley, which brought them out on the edge of the Orto del Castello that surrounded the castle. The castle itself looked no more ruined than it had first thing that morning. It had probably survived lots of earthquakes already, as well as rocks, arrows and cannonballs and anything else the town's enemies could think of throwing at it.

The gardens were dotted with people sitting or lying on the grass. Not far from the castle walls a couple of people were pitching a tent. The only sign of damage was in an ornamental fountain, where a stone dolphin in motion lay shattered in its basin. Water was still gushing out, overflowing the bowl and puddling on the ground.

Ben reached the fountain and splashed water over his face and head, then he cupped his hands under the outflow so that he could drink. The water was icy, and it helped to revive him and wash away the dirt of the earthquake.

As he waited for Carly to take her turn, he wondered whether it had been a good idea to drink the water. Something might have polluted it. Still, it was too late now. And he certainly felt better. So did Carly – as she straightened up, clean face shining out of hair that was still filthy, she started to smile again. She puffed her breath out hard as she shook sparkling drops of water from her hair and hands. 'That's better. OK, let's get moving.'

As they set off again, along the street beside the gardens, Ben heard a high-pitched screaming, and a moment later something cannoned into his legs from behind, almost knocking him over. He turned and saw a small girl. She was wearing only a cotton nightdress, and her feet were bare. Her face and hands were filthy, and she was sobbing, still clinging to Ben. She was repeating something over and over again in Italian.

'*Mammina! Mammina!*'

'What's the matter?' Ben spoke to Carly, not to the little girl. 'Does she want her mum? Do you know any Italian?'

'A bit.' Carly squatted down and put an

arm round the girl. 'What's wrong? *Che c'e?* Have you lost your mum?'

The little girl clutched at her and repeated, '*Mammina, mammina!*'

'Thought so,' Carly said to Ben, cuddling the little girl. 'Don't worry, love. We'll look after you. Do you know where you live? *Dove abiti tu?*'

The girl replied with a flood of Italian that left Carly shaking her head in bewilderment. Ben, whose Italian ran to 'please' and 'thank you' and not much else, didn't even try to make sense of it.

'We can't understand her,' he said to Carly. 'We'll have to find a policeman.'

Carly gave the little girl another hug. 'What's your name – hang on – *come ti chiami?*'

The little girl's screams had died down into gulping sobs. 'Francesca,' she said.

'Carly,' said Carly, pointing to herself. 'And that lump there is Ben.'

'What have I done?' Ben asked.

'Nothing,' Carly sighed. 'That's the trouble. Where's this policeman you were on about?'

Carly sat down on the low wall

surrounding the garden and lifted Francesca on to her lap while Ben looked around. He couldn't see a policeman anywhere.

Remembering that he had passed the police station when he was in the town the other day, he took a few paces back towards the centre, then he caught sight of a man standing at the nearest street corner. He was bare-headed, with his sleeves rolled up, his shabby clothes covered in dust, but Ben recognized his clothing as the remains of a policeman's uniform.

The policeman was talking to a dark-haired woman who was looking very upset as she explained something to him. He was scratching his head, shrugging, as if at a loss to answer her.

Trying to run, Ben hurried across the street and caught the policeman's arm. The policeman tried to shake him off, saying something irritably in Italian.

'No,' said Ben. 'Over here. Look. *Bambino,*' he added to the woman, with a sudden flash of inspiration.

The woman turned to look where he was pointing and the worry on her face was wiped away. '*Eccola!* Francesca!' she cried out.

She dashed across the street, and Francesca scrambled off Carly's lap and ran to meet her.

Her mother knelt beside her and hugged her. The policeman followed, said a few words and moved off, while Ben rejoined Carly. For all his tiredness, and his worry about his own parents, he felt something warm grow inside him. At least they'd done something to help, however tiny.

Holding her daughter by the hand, Francesca's mother came over to Carly and spoke to her in Italian. She was crying. Ben thought he knew what she was trying to say, though the only word he understood was *grazie* – thank you.

Carly raised her hands. 'Sorry, I don't understand. *Inglese*, OK? *Prego, prego.* It was a pleasure. *Arriverderci.*'

'*Arriverderci,*' Francesca said.

Her mother hugged Carly and Ben, still sobbing, and thanked them warmly.

'There,' Carly said, as they moved off from the scene. 'Doesn't that make you feel good?'

'You're all heart.' Ben grinned and ducked his head as Carly swiped at him. 'Let's get on.'

He led the way along the edge of the gardens. The warm feeling inside him soon froze to ice as he began to wonder again about his mum and dad. The collapse of the apartment building replayed itself in his mind like a slow-motion film, and he started to ask himself what he would do if they were badly hurt, or even dead.

CHAPTER SEVEN

Ben and Carly skirted the Orto del Castello until they found the street that led towards the resort. More cars were blocking it, and they tried another alley to work their way round. It was quieter here; there were tumbled walls and heaps of stone, but most of them looked as if they had been there for a long time. Eventually the alley led into another street, and this one they recognized, so they turned up the hill again towards the resort.

Leaving the town behind them, the road wound between the white walls of gardens and courtyards belonging to the last few houses.

A few paces ahead of Ben, Carly turned a corner and stopped. 'Oh, no!' Ben caught up with her and saw what she was staring at. A cypress tree by the side of the road had obviously been uprooted in the earthquake; it had smashed through the wall of the garden where it grew and had fallen across the road, to lie across the garden on the other side. A small red car, abandoned, was nosed up against the dark branches.

'We'll have to climb over it,' Ben said. 'It's not so bad.'

He edged past the car and plunged in among the branches, feathery at the outer ends, tougher and more like whips as he waded through them towards the trunk. The cypress needles had a warm, spicy smell. Twigs scratched his hands; he tried to shield his face as he hauled himself up and over the trunk, then half jumped, half slid down the other side. He turned round to give Carly a hand, but she was already following, and Ben pushed his way out of the branches to leave her space to jump down. They were across the last barrier – at least, Ben hoped it was the last – before reaching the resort and their parents.

The road grew steeper as it curled towards the resort. The sound of people crying out had been in the background all the while they were in the town; now it died away behind them, and in the new silence Ben could hear a bird singing. Did that mean it was really over?

His whole body was aching and it was hard to put one foot in front of the other as he toiled up the last of the slope. Head down, he kept his eyes fixed on the cracks in the surface of the road and the little clouds of dust that his footsteps threw up.

He heard Carly let out a long sigh. She had stopped and turned to look back at the town. Most of it was hidden by trees in their path and by a cloud of smoke and dust that hung in the air and turned the sunlight hazy. Ben remembered how peaceful it had seemed when he looked down from the balcony the night before.

'Come on,' he said.

The outer wall of the resort had crumbled and the wrought-iron gates were twisted and thrown down. Beyond them, however, flowers still edged the paths, and the first apartment blocks they passed looked almost normal. Except that usually by this time balcony doors would be open and people would be sunning themselves, or draping wet towels and swimming things over the rails. Now everything was shut up.

Carly's pace quickened, and Ben forced himself into a jog to keep up with her. Rounding the corner of the next block, they came to their own building.

The whole of the balcony wall had been sheared away and lay in mounds of rubble at the base of the building. Rooms were exposed to the open air, some of them with furniture poking out over the drop. Ben counted up five floors to his own apartment, but he could see nothing in the gap, no clue to where his parents might be.

At ground level, several people were clustered over the wreckage, working to heave away stones by hand. They looked like holidaymakers from the other apartments. There was no sign of any official rescue services and no equipment to help. Of course, Ben thought, with a sick feeling in his stomach, there'll be people buried under there. Even as he watched, two of the rescuers bent and lifted a limp body out of the rubble;

Ben couldn't see who it was, or even if the person was still alive.

Walking more slowly now, pushing back apprehension, he crossed to the edge of the wrecked area. Recognizing someone he'd met at the swimming pool, he grabbed the man's arm and asked, 'Have you seen –'

The man stared at him without recognizing him. His face was smeared with dust and he looked tired. He shook Ben's hand off and broke in on him: 'If you can't help, don't get in the way.' Then he went back to hauling stone.

Ben stood still, clenching his teeth, wanting to start yelling, 'Mum! Dad!' If he wasn't careful, he would be panicking like little Francesca in the town. He watched the rescuers for a minute, but none of them were the people he most wanted to see.

When he had himself under control again, he looked around for Carly. She was talking to a woman Ben did not recognize but, as Ben caught sight of them, they separated and Carly came to join him.

'She says there's a first-aid post in the clubhouse,' she told him. 'They're taking the injured down there. The phone lines are down so they can't ring for ambulances, but somebody went to the hospital on foot. I can't understand it,' she added. 'I'd expect to see some of them – your lot or mine.'

'Maybe they went somewhere together,' Ben said hopefully.

'Maybe.' Carly didn't sound convinced.

Ben started searching to see if their car was still there. The parking area was across the road from the apartment block. Only two cars were parked there; one had been badly damaged by flying chunks of masonry. Neither car belonged to his family, or to Carly's. He nudged Carly. 'Our cars aren't there.'

Carly glanced across at the parking area, and she seemed to brighten up a bit. 'Maybe they did go out.'

Now that the first shock of getting close up to the damage was over, Ben could get a better idea of what was going on. Teams of rescuers were heaving stones away to get down into the rubble. When they uncovered someone, they lifted the victim to the edge of the debris, from where other teams would carry him or her down to the path towards the clubhouse. The operation looked organized; all the rescuers were doing the best they could.

Ben continued to watch them, scanning the faces of the people they lifted out of the wreckage to see if one of them was his mum or dad. He was distracted from this when Carly grabbed his arm and tugged him forward.

'Ben – look!'

He followed her pointing hand. Across the heaps of stone, close to the building itself, they were uncovering a young man. He was tall and thin, and under its coating of dust his hair was dark.

Carly said, 'It's Tim!'

The rescuers laid Carly's brother down to await transport to the clubhouse. Carly scrambled over piles of rubble until she reached him, and she dropped to her knees by his side. Ben hung back a little.

Tim was lying on his back. His face and his clothes were streaked with white dust, and blood oozed from a cut on his forehead. One leg was at an awkward angle. His eyes were closed, but they fluttered open as Carly shook his shoulder gently and said, 'Tim! Tim!'

'Carly?' Tim's voice was blurred.

'Yes, it's me, Carly. Ben's here, too. Tim, what happened? Are you hurt?'

'Leg's broken, I think. And my head . . .' He tried to grin.

'Tim . . .' Carly reached for her brother's hand and clasped it. 'Tim, where are Mum and Dad?'

Tim's eyes closed again and he turned his head restlessly from one side to the other. Ben thought he was struggling to stay conscious. Being questioned wasn't what he needed.

'Tim, you have to tell us!' Carly was getting frantic.

Tim groaned and opened his eyes again.

'Not here,' he said, making a huge effort to tell the story properly. 'They went to the supermarket. Not back when the 'quake struck.'

'But – hang on.' Ben squatted down on his heels beside Tim. 'What about the first shock? Just after sunrise? Weren't they worried, or –'

'First shock?' Tim interrupted. 'What first shock?'

'They must have slept through it,' said Carly. 'What time did you get up, Tim?'

Tim gave another feeble grin.

'Not sunrise. Not all energetic like you.'

'Then they're probably OK,' said Carly. She sat back and thrust her hands through filthy, tangled hair. To Ben she sounded as if she was trying to convince herself. 'The supermarket's on the edge of town. They wouldn't have got mixed up in all that.'

She flapped a hand in the direction she and Ben had come from. Ben wondered if she was right. The supermarket might have collapsed while the Scotts were in it, or they might have crashed their car if they had been driving when the main shock struck. But he had the sense not to say anything; Carly knew as well as anyone what might have happened.

While they were talking, Ben kept looking around. Work on the damaged building continued. He still couldn't see his own mum or dad.

'Tim,' he began, 'have you seen —'

Tim didn't take any notice. He was explaining to Carly what had happened when the earthquake struck.

'I was on the balcony, reading. I tried to get in, but I couldn't stand. It felt as if the whole building was whipping about the sky. The noise was . . . like a plane going over. But it kept on, really loud. Then the balcony and the rest of the wall split off and crashed. I thought I'd had it.' He paused; his eyes half-closed, exhausted, but after a moment he went on, 'Something hit me, and everything went black. Then . . . light shining in my eyes. Don't remember . . . felt something heavy on my legs. Pain. So much pain. And then somebody was carrying me over here.' He sighed and closed his eyes again. His face was as white as the dust streaking it. Talking had worn him out.

'You were really lucky,' Carly said. She brushed some dust from her brother's forehead. 'I guess they'll get an ambulance up here sooner or later. Hang on in there, ugly.'

Ben looked around again. The rescuers had just uncovered the limp body of a woman, and were carrying her towards them. She wasn't his mum. As they laid her down carefully beside Tim, Ben grabbed the arm of the woman nearest him.

'Have you seen my mum and dad?' Almost as soon as he spoke he realized how stupid that sounded. 'Mr and Mrs Fletcher? He's tall, fair – mum has red hair, and . . .' His voice died away.

'I don't think so,' said the other man. He spoke with a heavy German accent. 'Perhaps your mother and father had gone out somewhere.' He glanced at the piles of debris, and though he didn't say any more Ben knew what he was thinking. *Or they're still under there.*

Ben tried to smile. 'Maybe. Thanks.'

The man rested a hand on his shoulder for a second and then went back to the job.

'You reckon they went to Venice?' Carly said.

Ben shrugged. 'Don't know.'

It was possible, he thought, but unlikely. If he knew his mum, she and his dad would have been waiting, to give him an unforgettable welcome when he got back. And they couldn't still be inside the building. What was left was more or less undamaged; they wouldn't have been hurt, or not so badly that they couldn't get out. And their car was gone. So where were they now?

'Tim?' he said. He hated to disturb Carly's brother when he was tired and in pain, but he had to know. He shook Tim's shoulder again, and Tim opened his eyes. 'Tim, did you see my mum and dad? Did you hear them going out?'

Tim shook his head.

Carly said, 'They might have gone to the supermarket with Mum and Dad and Sara.'

'Sara?' Tim's voice was a terrified croak. He reached out and gripped Carly's wrist. 'Carly, Sara wasn't with mum and dad. She was with me!'

CHAPTER EIGHT

Ben and Carly stared at Tim. All the colour had drained from Carly's face. She pushed her brother back as he started struggling to get up.

'Tell me,' she insisted.

'I was babysitting,' Tim explained. 'Sara was asleep in the carrycot, in Mum and Dad's room. Carly, get off – I've got to go and find her!'

'With a broken leg? Tim, stop being stupid. We'll do it.'

Ben was already on his feet, looking up at the remains of the apartment block. 'Keep calm,' he said. 'She'll be OK. We just have to fetch her, that's all.'

He set off towards the entrance. Carly passed him, sprinting, only to be intercepted by one of the rescuers working in the middle of the rubble.

'Where do you think you're going?'

Carly pointed. 'In there.'

'Oh no, you're not. That building could collapse any minute. Nobody goes any closer than they have to.'

'But I have to! My little sister's in there!'

The man relaxed and patted her shoulder. 'No she isn't, love. We've checked, top to bottom. Nobody's left in there.'

'She's only a baby,' Ben said. 'In a carrycot. Are you sure somebody brought her out?'

'Sure as I can be. Look, we're using the clubhouse as a first-aid post. Somebody must have taken her over there.'

'But you haven't seen her?' Carly persisted.

'No.' The man was starting to look impatient. 'But I've told you, the building's been thoroughly checked.'

'Let me go and make sure. I'll only be a minute.'

'No.' The man's face reddened with anger. 'We can't have more lives at risk. Go down to the clubhouse and let us get on with the job.

There'll be other people still under there, you know.' He wiped the palms of his hands on his trousers, turned away and started hauling on the nearest lump of stone, but Ben could see he still had an eye on them. There were other people working, too, between them and the entrance. Carly was measuring the distance with her eye, but after a moment she shrugged. 'C'mon, Ben. Let's check the clubhouse.'

They walked away, but as soon as they were out of earshot Carly muttered, 'He doesn't really know where she is. Ben, if Sara's not in the clubhouse, I'm going back there and I'm going to get in somehow.'

The clubhouse was a low, white building curving in a semi-circle around a swimming pool. As well as the resort reception area, there was a bar and restaurant, a sauna and a games room.

As they approached, Ben could see a crack running the whole length of the pool. The water had drained away, apart from a few centimetres of mud in the bottom. The diving board had collapsed into it. Ben remembered swimming there with Carly the day before, showing off his dives.

The clubhouse building itself looked relatively undamaged. The doors of the restaurant stood open. Inside, the staff were serving drinks and sandwiches to a group of battered-looking people who could be rescuers or victims. Ben's heart leapt, but a quick glance told him that his parents were not among them. He cast one longing glance at the food, but there was no time to stop.

Beyond the restaurant, the doors to the games room also stood open. Exercise bikes and training machines had been pushed aside around the walls, and still figures lay sleeping in cocoons of bedding on the floor.

Carly and Ben went in. A woman who had been stooping over the nearest of the survivors got up and came over to them.

'Are the ambulances here yet?' she asked.

Ben shook his head.

'Then it's about time,' the woman went on. She was small and dark, about his mother's age. 'I'm a trained nurse, but there's only so much I can do by myself. What do you want?' She sounded sharp to begin with, but then her voice softened. 'Are you looking for someone?'

'My baby sister,' Carly said, at the same time as Ben said, 'My mum and dad.'

The nurse gave a tight smile that Ben thought might easily have turned to tears. 'What you see is what we've got.' She indicated the line of victims behind her. 'Have a look.'

Ben walked along the line, but it took only a minute to check that none of them was his mum or his dad.

Carly continued, 'My sister was probably in a carrycot. Is she here?'

The nurse shook her head and put a hand sympathetically on Carly's arm. 'I haven't seen her. Just a minute.' She went to the door and called, 'Giovanni! *Venga qui!*'

One of the restaurant waiters came into the room. The nurse spoke to him rapidly in Italian; he replied, then went out again.

'He hasn't seen her either,' the nurse explained. 'But he'll ask around. If she's found, he'll bring her here.'

'Thank you.' Carly swallowed. 'She was in the building when the balconies collapsed.'

'I'm sorry.' The nurse gave her a hug. 'But it doesn't mean the worst has happened, you know. Some people out there went into other apartments to rest. They could have taken your sister with them. She might be anywhere.'

Carly nodded. In an expressionless voice, she said, 'Come on, Ben.'

Ben thanked the nurse and followed Carly out. Beside the wrecked swimming pool, Carly whirled around and said, 'She's still in there! I know she is!'

'She might not be.' Ben was trying to sound reasonable and not let himself give way to panic. 'Maybe my mum and dad went and got her.' He liked that idea; it was really comforting. 'Like the nurse said, they could be in somebody else's apartment.'

Carly planted her feet apart and put her hands on her hips. 'I don't believe it, Ben. If they'd got her, they'd be looking for us – and for Tim. They wouldn't just sit around drinking coffee!' She spun around and gazed at the other buildings. 'Besides, how long do you think it would take to check? You heard what that man said. Our building could go any minute. With Sara inside it. Ben, I *know* she's in there! And I'm going to get her out. That man isn't going to stop me, and neither is anybody else.'

She started striding up the path towards the building. Ben watched her retreating figure, then hurried after her to catch her up.

'OK,' he said. 'I'm coming with you.'

At the entrance to the pool area they had to step aside to let two rescuers pass. They were carrying Tim on a makeshift stretcher, on their way to the first-aid post. Carly bent over her brother, but he was unconscious again.

'He'll be OK.' Ben tried to encourage her. 'That nurse was really nice.'

Carly nodded. 'But he needs a hospital. They all do.' She shook her head, as if to clear it. 'Anyway, we have to think of Sara now.'

'Right – but Carly, listen. Don't just go charging up there. They'll keep us out for sure if you do that. Let's take it slowly – suss it out first.'

Carly looked dubious for a moment, and then gave him a brief nod. Her voice suddenly choking, she said, 'I keep remembering how her crying bugged me last night.' She wiped away a couple of tears with the palm of her hand, leaving streaks across her face. 'Why are we standing around? Let's go.'

The path led away from the pool, winding between beds of flowers and shrubs. Here there was not much damage and in the hot sun the plants were giving off a heady scent. Ben could almost pretend that the whole of the day so far had been a nightmare he had dreamt in his sleep, and he would wake to find the apartment building undamaged and his parents waiting.

But if it was a nightmare, he was still living it.

Rescuers were still working at the foot of the building, between Carly and Ben and the entrance. Carly paused in the shelter of the last clump of bushes, and murmured, 'If they see us, they'll chase us off again.'

'There's a back entrance,' Ben said. 'They use it for cleaning and stuff.'

Carly flashed him a grin, her optimism returning. 'Right. Let's do it!'

Carefully they worked their way round, cutting across the shrubs with their heads ducked below the level of the branches. They hoped that no one would see them and ask them what they were doing.

A couple of minutes later, they were standing looking at the back door to the apartments, a few metres away. On this side, only a few spidery cracks in the white façade showed that the building was damaged. No one was around.

'Let's hope it's not locked,' Carly said.

Ben gave a last look back and forth. 'Now!'

They ran across the stretch of open lawn. Ben flung himself at the door, jerking at the handle. The door swung inwards. Carly followed Ben inside. They found themselves in a small, tiled foyer with a flight of stairs leading upwards in front of them. Everything was silent. The air smelt of dust.

No one was yelling at them from outside. Ben realized with relief that they must have got in unseen. Cautiously he put his foot on the bottom stair.

'C'mon,' Carly urged him from behind.

They began to climb, carefully and silently. Ben could not help feeling that any loud noise or sudden movement might bring the whole building crashing down around them.

Halfway up the first flight, he paused as a long, soft groaning noise swept through the block. Swallowing, he glanced back at Carly. 'It's going to go.'

'Hurry, then.'

He went on. He knew that there was still a risk of further aftershocks – even the smallest tremors could destroy buildings already weakened by the big 'quake. Thinking about it made it harder still for him to put one foot in front of the other, step after step.

Near the top of the first flight of stairs he half turned to Carly and said, 'I've got to check our apartment. Mum and Dad might . . .' He couldn't finish. Even though the rescuer had said the building was empty, he had to make sure.

Carly nodded, and they climbed on.

On every landing, a fire door separated the staircase from the main part of the building. Ben counted how many floors they had passed until they came to the fifth. Then he pushed through the fire door and stood on the main landing.

The floor was covered in slivers of glass from shattered windows. A picture of St Mark's Square in Venice had fallen off the wall and smashed. Opposite, the door of his family's apartment stood wide open. Ben halted.

'Why'd they leave the door open?' he asked.

'Don't suppose they did,' Carly replied, pushing past him and padding carefully across the littered floor. 'You heard that man – they checked the building. They must have keys at reception.'

Ben caught her up and peered cautiously through the door. 'Mum? Dad?' He did not dare raise his voice. He walked along the narrow entrance hall and tried the first door, which was his own bedroom. At first it stuck, as if the door frame had shifted, but as Ben pushed harder it flew open and he almost fell into the room. It was empty.

Carly was checking the bathroom. Again nothing, except for the regular sound of water dripping from a cracked pipe and puddling in a widening pool on the floor.

Ben went on to his parents' room. Here it looked as if the window had burst inwards, spraying shards of glass over everything. Ben tried the wardrobe, then squatted down to peer under the bed, but no one was there.

'Hey!' Carly called to him softly. 'Come and look at this!'

She was standing in the kitchen doorway. This was the part of the apartment where the wreckage was worst. Kitchen cupboards had fallen off the walls, scattering their contents over the kitchen surfaces and the floor. Everything was covered in coffee and pasta and a sticky mixture of wine and honey and tomato sauce. Pots and pans and smashed glasses looked like drifting flotsam on a sea of sludge. The fridge had migrated to the other side of the room, still tethered to the wall by its flex. The cooker was poking out from its place under the kitchen unit, in the midst of a tangle of wires.

'Don't touch that,' Ben warned Carly.

'Hey, I'm not stupid!'

The only other room in the apartment was the sitting room, exposed to the open air where the balcony wall had sheared off. Ben took one look at the smashed remains of the furniture and backed away.

'Where are they?' he asked, not expecting a reply. They might have been sitting on the balcony, he added silently. They might have been watching for me to come back. They might be buried now.

Carly led the way back on to the landing. This time they took the main stairs, up to the Scotts' apartment on the floor above.

Ben felt they needed to tread softly and try

not to breathe. He listened out for noise and signs of life but heard nothing – only the occasional moan of stressed brickwork and groaning foundations. He couldn't help thinking that, if Sara was still there, they would hear her crying.

When the noise began, they optimistically hoped it would be a rescue vehicle of some sort.

It was a low, grinding sound that gradually grew louder.

As they reached the sixth floor, Ben glanced out of the window, expecting to see a lorry or a rescue helicopter. Instead, he caught a glimpse of the ground below, and people running in all directions, away from the building. At the same moment, the floor rippled and bucked under his feet.

It was another aftershock.

'No!' Carly yelled.

'Come back! We've got to –'

'I'm getting Sara!'

Carly threw herself at the open door of her own apartment, lost her balance and fell full length on the landing. Ben managed to stay upright by clinging to the banister at the top of the stairs. He felt as if he was trying to hold on to the mast of a sailing boat in a gale. He wanted to turn and run, but the stairs behind him looked more like one of the scary rides at the water park.

'Carly – hang on to something!' he shouted.

Carly was still trying to crawl forward to the door of the apartment. The smooth floor offered nothing for her to cling to, and she kept slipping from side to side as it tilted. She was still yelling, but Ben couldn't make out the words in the roar that assaulted his ears as the building finally gave way.

The banister was ripped from his grasp. He was flung across the floor, rolled over and over, and then was tossed against a wall with a force that knocked all the breath out of him. Briefly he saw Carly, a tangle of arms and legs a metre or so away. As he felt the floor give way beneath him, Ben reached out for her. He was plunging downwards, in a cascade of wood and stone and choking dust. He tried to scream. Then something hit him on the head. Pain split the world in two, and he pitched soundlessly into the black space between.

CHAPTER NINE

Somebody was using a hammer and chisel to hack their way into Ben's head. He muttered, 'Get off.' His voice sounded thick and his tongue was too big for his mouth.

He tried to open his eyes. He could see nothing. His eyes were stinging; he shut them tight against the pain and felt tears squeezing out between the lids. He tried to raise his hand to rub at them but found that something was pinning him down.

Panic lanced through him. He wanted to thrash out, to free himself, but he couldn't move. He shouted, 'Help! Help me! Get me out!'

His cries gave way to a spasm of coughing. The grit in his mouth tasted disgusting. He coughed and spat, and coughed again. He tried a second time to open his eyes, blinking away the dust. He could still see nothing but darkness.

Panting, he lay still. Gradually he began to remember what had happened. The search for Sara in the abandoned building. The devastation in his own apartment. The building collapsing. 'Carly!' His voice rasped in his throat. 'Carly!'

There was no reply.

He felt himself shuddering all over. *Get hold of yourself*, he thought. *Think.*

Gradually, the worst of his panic ebbed. He was able to take stock of where he was and what he must do next. In the darkness he could see nothing so he started to work out what he could feel.

To begin with, he was alive.

That was an immediate bonus.

His head ached savagely; he vaguely remembered something hitting it. But it was definitely working.

His eyes. He couldn't see. Was he blind, or was it so dark because he was buried deep, too deep for light to filter through? Ben didn't want to think about either of those possibilities.

He could still speak, even though his throat hurt and his tongue was swollen. He would have committed murder for a drink of water. And he could hear his own voice, though everything else was quiet.

The only real pain he could feel was in his head, even though the rest of his body felt like a single giant ache. He hoped that meant he wasn't too badly injured.

Ben began trying to move, cautiously this time. His left hand was free, enough to grope around anyway, so he could try to make sense of where he was lying. Underneath him was a layer of loose stone, but if he dug his fingers into it he felt something more solid, something smooth like a tiled floor. Trying to reach up, he could touch more stones and he felt them shift. There was a pattering noise, as if he had disturbed something. He froze, fear flaring up again. But when the pattering died away, Ben felt as if the weight pinning him down was slightly less.

Cautiously he tried moving his hand again,

this time pressing against the ground to see if he could raise himself at all.

The soft cascade of small stones began again, and it grew as Ben heaved himself up. A sharp pain stabbed him in the ribs. Wincing, he collapsed, breathing hard, but the weight on top of him was definitely less now, and he found he could move his other arm and flex his legs. He had a mental picture of himself buried in a mound of gravel and loose debris that was gradually giving way as he tried to move.

Though the air was thick with dust, he had no real trouble breathing. He must be lying in a cavity somewhere in the ruins of the building. So what was making the cavity? he asked himself, and then he wished he hadn't. What's stopping me from being squashed flat?

A picture came into his mind of tonnes of stone over his head, joists and water pipes, fittings and furniture, all ready to come crashing down if he made a wrong move. He lay very still for a long time after that, until he managed to push the picture away.

While he was lying there, he tried to decide what to do. There had been rescuers, pulling people out from the first lot of debris, when the balconies gave way. He had seen them running, in fear of the whole building collapsing. There must still be some people out there who were trying to help.

He imagined rescuers up above him, lifting stones from the pile of wreckage. That comforted him for a while. Then he realized that the job was far bigger than that; they would need cranes or something to shift the massive weight over his head.

No one was out there except people from the resort itself. So far Ben had seen nothing of official rescue services except for the police by the bridge. The local ones would be occupied in the town, he supposed. And it would take a while for others to come from further afield. He had no idea how far away the earthquake would have been felt. He could be in for a long wait.

On top of that came another thought, even more chilling.

They checked the building. They think it's empty. Nobody knows I'm in here.

Peering into the darkness was making his eyes ache. Even though he knew it was hopeless, he couldn't help trying to see what was around him. He raised a hand to rub across his face, blinked, and blinked again. Very faintly, he could see the outline of his hand.

Somewhere over to his right was a yellowish glow. Something black slashed across it; as Ben made sense of what he could see, he realized it was a huge concrete joist, tilted at an angle. The light-source, whatever it was, lay beyond it.

Ben shouted, 'Hi! Anybody there?'

'Ben? Ben, is that you?' It was Carly's voice.

A flood of relief washed over Ben. Though he hadn't let himself put the thought into words, he had been assuming all along that Carly was dead.

'Over here!'

There was a slithering noise. Ben gritted his teeth, expecting to hear the groan of the shifting building, but everything was still. A moment later, Carly's head appeared beneath the joist. Her face was white with a coating of dust, and her hair was tangled round it. She was dragging herself forward on her stomach, one hand clutching a tiny torch.

'You OK, Ben?' she asked.

'Think so.'

In the torchlight, Ben could see where he was. As he had thought, he was half buried in a mound of dirt and small stones. Above him, the concrete joist was balanced on top of another that met it at an angle; something dark and heavy loomed above them on the edge of the wavering circle of light.

He managed to sit up, scraping at the debris that had buried him. Pain stabbed into his ribs again; he guessed he had broken one or at least had bruised it very badly. A gooey trickle of blood extended down across his temple. He let his fingers gently find a congealed cut on the right side of his head. Apart from that, everything else seemed to work OK.

'What about you?' he asked Carly.

She gave him a tight grin. 'Right arm's not too good.' She was carrying the torch in her left. 'Still, it's not all bad. Dad can't expect me to write my holiday project now.'

Ben couldn't help but smile. If you had to be buried under a ten-storey building with nobody to get you out, Carly was a good person to have with you.

Carly snapped off the light. 'Saving the battery,' she said through the darkness. 'It's only my key ring.' After a moment, she added, 'What do you think we should do?'

'I don't know. They don't know we're here.'

'Yeah. I'd worked that one out, too.'

'We could try shouting,' Ben suggested.

They tried, for several minutes, until their voices started to give way. Ben's throat felt raw and he was shaking with exhaustion. They both lay quiet at last. No reply came as a result of their shouting, no sound at all apart from an occasional scraping or pattering sound as the building settled.

'I hate that,' Carly said. 'I keep thinking the whole lot's going to go.'

Ben reached out for her and found her hand groping for his. They lay still for a long time, hands tightly clasped. After a while, Carly said, 'Back there, where I came from, there's this sort of dark space. It might lead somewhere.'

Ben groaned. He was terrified at the thought of leaving this refuge and perhaps ending up somewhere worse, somewhere that would give way and crush them. But he said, 'You want to try it?'

'No.' A long pause. Then, 'Maybe we should. While we're still strong enough.'

Neither of them moved. Eventually Ben said, 'Let's wait a while. We'll try that way later, if nobody comes.'

'They might well not come. Ben, were you unconscious?'

'Yes.'

'So was I. We don't know how long for. It could be night out there. They could have given up. Maybe –'

Ben gripped her hand more tightly. His free hand was clenched into a fist, fingernails digging into his palm. He made himself speak quietly. 'We don't know that. Our parents will keep looking for us.' *If they can*, he added silently.

He heard a long sigh from Carly, then he felt her relax. 'Yeah. Sure.'

Time passed.

Ben wanted to sleep, but he knew that was the one thing he mustn't do. If they both slept, they might not hear the rescuers when they came. No harm in resting, though, he thought. Get some strength up to try Carly's black hole. Close my eyes . . .

Abruptly he came back to consciousness as Carly jerked his hand.

'Ben Fletcher, you snore!' she accused him.

'No I don't!'

'Oh, yes, you do. Like a pneumatic drill. Let's sing or something, to keep ourselves awake.' She cleared her throat. '*Row, row, row your boat . . .*'

'Ouch!' Ben said. 'Flat.'

'I know. Never could sing a note.' Suddenly she collapsed into giggles. 'Ben, I feel really stupid!'

'Let's play games, then. I spy with my little eye . . . something beginning with r.'

'Rubble!' Carly said immediately.

'Correct!'

Carly giggled again, as Ben had hoped. The sound warmed him. Nothing was quite as bad when you had somebody to share it with.

'OK, let's play Beethoven,' she suggested.

'Sorry. Got no piano.'

'No, it's a game, stupid!' Carly jerked on his hand again. 'You think of a person – somebody in history, or the news, or out of a book – and then the other player has to guess who you are. OK, I've got somebody. Ask me questions.'

'Er . . .' Ben couldn't believe he was playing party games under one hundred tonnes of stone. 'Are you male or female?'

'I can only answer yes or no, idiot.'

'You didn't say that! OK, are you male?'

'No.'

'Female?'

Carly sighed. 'Doh! What do you think? *Yes*.'

'Are you real?'

'Yes.'

'Are you dead?'

Carly muttered, 'Not yet – but yes, in the game,' and Ben realized that this might not have been the best question to ask. He couldn't think of any more questions. He could just feel Carly getting more and more impatient. A woman who was dead . . . somebody in history maybe. 'Are you a queen?'

'Yes.'

'Elizabeth the First?'

'No.'

Ben wasn't sure he knew any more queens. He started to say, 'Er . . . are you –' when Carly pulled at his hand again.

'I'm thinking,' he protested.

'No, Ben. Listen!'

Ben froze. He listened, but he could hear nothing. Maybe all Carly had heard was the building shifting. 'I can't hear anything.'

'Listen!' she hissed.

Then he heard it too. A thin cry, trickling through the wreckage from the direction behind Carly. A faint and unhappy wailing. It stopped, then began again.

'It's Sara!' Carly whispered. 'It's Sara! It has to be. It's Sara. She's alive!'

CHAPTER TEN

The sound of baby Sara's anguished cries continued to drift in the darkness through the pockets of air towards Ben and Carly.

'We have to get to her,' Carly said urgently.

She released Ben's hand and snapped on her keyring light again. Ben was dazzled after so long in the thick blackness. He blinked. When his vision had cleared, he saw Carly's face, alive with hope again, under the angle of the joist.

'She's back there,' Carly said, 'in that space I told you about. She must be.'

'Just take it easy,' Ben said. 'We don't want to disturb anything.'

'Right.' Carly began wriggling backwards, very slowly and carefully. 'Ben, let me turn around, then you follow, OK?'

'OK.'

Carly jack-knifed her body in the space, so that she was facing the way she had come. Her right arm was dragging uselessly; she gasped with pain as it moved. Her face set, she muttered, 'Broken, I guess.'

Ben could do nothing to help her, only wait until she was in position and began inching towards the faint cries that still came out of the darkness beyond. When she had cleared the gap, he started to pull himself along the ground after her, gritting his teeth against the pain as he jolted his aching ribs.

On the other side of the joist was another clear space. The keyring torch wasn't powerful enough to show Ben what was holding the wreckage up, and he decided he would rather not know. He just kept his eyes fixed on the tiny glow in Carly's hand.

Soon he could see the dark gap she had told him about. He hadn't thought it would be so small; it was like a burrow that was hardly big enough for a decent-sized rabbit.

He wasn't sure he could make himself go in there. But now he had come this far, he could be sure that was where the baby's cries were coming from.

Carly glanced back at him. 'Come on,' she said. 'When I go in, you won't be able to see. Make sure you can follow.'

Ben knew this wasn't the time to have second thoughts. He dragged himself across the littered floor until his head was on a level with Carly's feet. The hole gaped beside her head. Ben could tell that Carly didn't like the look of it either. She started to edge forward and nearly dropped the torch; it was hard for her to manage it and move along with only one good hand.

'Let me go first,' Ben said.

Carly opened her mouth to protest, but gave up and shifted to one side, holding out the torch for Ben. Ben took it, grinned at her, and thrust his head and shoulders into the hole before he could think any more about it.

The thread of sound from Sara guided him forward, inching along with one hand pressed under his body and the other extended with the torch in it. Its light showed him the walls of the tunnel; they looked like close-packed, splintered wood, as if they had once been doors or furniture. He could hear Carly shuffling behind him, bumping into his shoes. At the end of the tunnel was another dark hole.

The passageway only stretched for another metre or so. Ben guessed that his head was poking out at the far end before his feet had disappeared at the opening. But it seemed a very long metre; the roof was very close to his unprotected head and back. Ben began shaking with relief as he pulled himself out into another and larger space.

Torchlight glimmered on a tangle of metal pipes above his head that stretched to the ground along one side. At the far side of the space was a jumble of furniture, including a bed and a number of smashed chairs. The crying was much louder now, but Ben could still not see any sign of Sara.

Behind him, he heard Carly's muffled voice. 'Let me out, will you?'

'Sorry.' Ben moved away from the mouth of the hole. There was space to sit up, so he could hold the torch for Carly and help her out.

She let her breath out as she scrabbled free

and struggled to her knees. 'That was awful.'
Looking around, she asked, 'Where's Sara?'

'I don't know.'

The wailing stopped, started, stopped
again. Ben thought it was coming from the
heap of furniture at the other side of the
space. He started to crawl across to it.

'Sara! Sara!' he called.

'You're not calling the dog,' Carly
grumbled behind him.

Reaching the furniture, Ben examined it
before he touched anything. One wrong
move could bring the whole lot down and
crush Sara if she was underneath. The bed
was the key, he thought, that was keeping
everything else in place. Whatever else he did,
he must make sure that stayed put.

'That's our bed!' Carly exclaimed. 'Mum's
and Dad's, I mean.' She grabbed at Ben. 'Ben,
that's where she is! In the 'quake, the carrycot
must have slid under the bed. That's why they
never found her when they checked the
building. She was under the bed, and she's still
under it!'

'OK,' said Ben. 'Keep calm. Hold the
torch.'

He handed the keyring back to Carly,

refusing to accept the evidence before his eyes that the faint light was growing fainter. He had told Carly to keep calm, but he was far from calm himself as he tackled the heap of furniture.

Very carefully, moving it only a centimetre at a time, he pulled away a chair that was wedged in the gap under the bed. Sara's crying suddenly got louder.

'Sara, it's all right!' Carly said. 'We're coming.'

There still wasn't enough space for Ben to reach under the bed. He worked at a stool that was jammed there, its upholstered top caught up on something. When it gave way with a tearing sound, and the stool popped out into his arms, he flinched, expecting the whole pile to collapse.

Nothing. Ben breathed again. He reached into the space beneath the bed. His fingers met a hard wall of ribbed fabric and, after a minute's groping, a handle. He pulled gently. The object slid forward, and caught.

'Got her, but she's stuck.'

Without thinking about the danger, he plunged his head into the gap. He was blocking the light with his own shoulders.

Groping, he found the obstruction, something small and squashy like a cushion, and passed it out behind him. Now that it was freed, the carrycot slid forward again when he tugged at it. As he freed himself and dragged the carrycot out with him, the whole pile of furniture seemed to sigh, and the bed flopped down on the heap beneath it.

Ben and Carly had no time to worry about that. Carly's face was streaked with tears as she bent over Sara's carrycot, gently brushing scraps of rubbish away from her sister's face. Sara's quilt was pushed to one side. At first the baby lay tightly curled up, with her arms and legs tucked into her body, but at Carly's touch she began waving and kicking feebly, and her mouth opened, shapeless, as she howled. Dust and splinters had fallen into the cot and got smeared over Sara's face and caught in her wispy hair. Miraculously, she seemed to be unhurt; at least, there were no obvious injuries.

Carly said, 'Pick her up.'

'Who, me? I don't know what to do for a baby.'

Carly sighed. 'You've got two good arms. Just pick her up, OK? Give her a cuddle.'

Awkwardly, feeling that Sara would come apart in his hands, Ben lifted her out of the cot. Her wailing died away to hiccuping.

'Hey, she likes me!' he said. He brushed away the worst of the debris from her baby suit and disentangled the splinters in her hair. 'She feels – sort of squashy,' he said. There was a pungent smell, as well. 'I reckon she wants a clean nappy.'

'Tough,' said Carly. 'That's the least of our worries.' She rested the torch on a ledge in the pile of debris and tipped up the carrycot with her good hand so she could scrape out the mess inside. 'What she really needs is a drink.'

'Don't we all.' Ben wished Carly hadn't said that. His mouth felt like a dustbowl. 'Hey, baby, don't cry.'

Sara had started to wail again, more quietly this time, but nevertheless it was a distinctly unhappy sound. Ben jogged her up and down. After a minute or two she stuck her thumb in her mouth, dropped her head on his shoulder, and went to sleep.

'Lay her down,' Carly said, setting the carrycot upright again. 'If she'll sleep for a bit we can find out if there's a way out through here.'

Ben put Sara down in the carrycot, and Carly tucked the quilt around her. Once Sara was settled, Carly held the torch again while Ben investigated the hollow behind the pile of furniture. It looked as if most of the tangled pipes met there, and they led off into a narrow tunnel quite like the one they had already come through.

Ben looked doubtfully at the hole. 'I could give it a try,' he said, knowing he didn't sound keen.

'You want the torch?'

'OK.'

Holding the light in front of him, he got down on his stomach and wriggled forward. This time he couldn't see anything ahead except the twisting pipes. He managed to pull himself along for a couple of metres, but the space was getting smaller all the time. Ben felt like a cork being rammed into the neck of a bottle. He could feel the tunnel roof scraping along his back. The floor under him was growing damp, as if water was seeping out from somewhere.

Eventually he had to admit defeat. The largest of the pipes made a right-angled turn straight in front of him, blocking off the remainder of the space. There was no way forward.

He rested for a minute, breathing hard and feeling sweat trickling under his clothes. Then he started to push himself backwards. His feet scrabbled against the ground. He could move his arms only a centimetre or two to get a purchase and push. The roof and walls pressed in on him. He was stuck.

For a minute he lay still again, fighting back panic. If he started screaming and thrashing around, he was finished. He found it hard to breathe. Was he blocking the air-supply with his own body?

'Carly?' he called. 'Carly, can you hear me?'

There was no reply. Ben pushed again, and thought he felt himself shift slightly. Again. Push. Again. A hand fastened round his ankle and tugged hard; he slid several centimetres over the rough ground and found himself back in the wider part of the tunnel. Rapidly he scrambled backwards and pushed himself out into the space beside Carly again.

Panting, he sat up and put his head in his hands. 'That was nasty.'

'No good?' Carly asked.

'You could say that.'

When he had recovered slightly, he held up the torch and looked around the rest of their prison. There was no other way out except for the hole they had come in by. Ben supposed he could go back to where he had first recovered consciousness, and explore more thoroughly there, but he had taken all he could of narrow tunnels for the time being.

'Put the light out,' Carly said.

Ben clicked off the torch, admitting what neither of them had said, that it was no use looking for a way out. Darkness surged around them again; out of it Ben could hear Sara snuffling restlessly in her cot, and then Carly's voice. 'Let's call for help again.'

'We'll wake the baby.'

'Then she can help. She's really good at screaming.'

They tried again, together, and after a minute Sara woke up and joined in as well. But it was no use. There were no sounds from outside, nothing to tell them that anyone was close enough to hear them.

'I can't keep this up,' Carly said at last. Her voice sounded rough, and it gave way to a spasm of coughing. Sara went on screaming for a minute or two, but her cries soon died away as well.

'We need to bang something,' Ben said. 'That's easier.'

He switched on the torch again; by now it was obvious that the light was almost spent. He shivered at the thought of sitting in the darkness and knowing he couldn't put a light on when he wanted it. He wasn't sure how long he could go on like that.

Quickly he crawled across to the heap of furniture and tugged out a splintered chair-leg. Using it like a club, he whacked the largest of the pipes alongside him. The sound rang out like a gong, and Sara started to cry again.

'Shhh!' Carly murmured, reaching into the cot to pat her sister. 'Ben, that's great. Keep going.'

Ben swung the chair-leg again. He was so tired that it was an effort to strike the pipe very hard at all, but still it was easier than trying to shout. He switched the light off again. The sound rolled out in the tiny space.

He struck five times and waited, listening for any sign that someone had heard him.

Nothing. Another five, and wait. Another –

'Listen!' said Carly.

Ben let the last blow fall. As the noise died away, he thought he could hear a faint scratching; he wasn't sure of the direction. Then it stopped. Almost frantic, he lashed out at the pipe again.

The noise was repeated, louder now.

Carly exclaimed, 'Yes, Ben! Yes!'

Ben began to beat a quicker, quieter rhythm on the pipe. Something to guide their rescuers to where they were, if there really were rescuers out there. He hardly dared to believe it.

Then he realized that he could just make out Carly's face. His friend was sitting beside the carrycot, her head raised to listen, an enormous grin splitting her face. But the torch was still switched off. Light was getting in to them from somewhere else.

Carly realized it at the same moment. 'Ben, they're coming!' she said, and began to call out, 'Here! We're over here!'

Ben kept up his drumroll banging on the pipe. Another, deeper rumble joined them. He heard a voice call, 'Careful!' as real, bright daylight flooded into their prison from the tunnel he had explored earlier. Tears flooded down his face, from the brilliance or the dust, or simply from relief. The sound of moving rubble filled the space.

Then someone called out, 'Ben? Carly? Are you in there?' and he thought his heart would stop, he was so thankful to hear those words.

It was his father's voice.

CHAPTER ELEVEN

'**D**ad?' Ben croaked. 'Dad, is that you?' Ben shivered and his limbs turned to jelly as a wave of relief flooded through him.

Carly called out too. 'We're here! And Sara – we've got Sara!'

'Thank God!' John Fletcher's voice again. 'Keep still. We're coming.'

There was more noise of shifting stone from the outside. Ben felt fresher air moving against his face. He took in great gulps of it. The daylight strengthened. Then another voice, one he didn't recognize, said, 'Can you hand the baby out first?'

Ben pushed Sara's cot over to the gap and

into the tunnel made by the pipes. By now there was a ragged hole at the far end where the light was coming from, and he could see blurred faces at the other end. He lost sight of them as he pushed the cot forward.

He had to follow it, still pushing, into the tunnel again, but before he reached the place where he had got stuck the time before, someone grabbed the cot from the far side and pulled it out and away. In its place, Ben saw his father, reaching out to him.

Ben held out a hand; John Fletcher gripped his wrist and pulled. Ben scrabbled with his feet and his free hand, and suddenly he was sliding forward, out into the air. His dad gripped his arms and helped him to find his feet on loose debris that shifted beneath him.

He had emerged from the side of the collapsed apartment building, several metres above ground level. Next to him, Graham Scott was already halfway inside the hole, reaching in for his elder daughter.

Ben's dad helped him to climb down over tilted blocks of stone and splintered wood. When he reached the ground, Ben's knees gave way and he sank down, resting his head in his hands. He was shuddering all over and didn't think he would ever be able to stop. Then somebody wrapped their arms round him and squeezed. He heard his mum in his ear saying, 'Ben – Ben, are you all right?'

He looked up. Marian Fletcher was crouching beside him. Her face was white and worried, but she was unhurt. Ben said, 'Mum, I'm really sorry,' and then he hugged her back, and choked out a sob against her shoulder.

The stabbing pain in his ribs roused him. He pulled away from his mum's arms and said, 'I think I've cracked a rib or something.'

Looking up, he saw Carly's dad helping her out of the hole in the wreckage. From the outside, the apartment building looked like a collapsed house of cards, the separate floors still visible as if they had just folded up and dropped straight down. Ben shivered again at the thought of all that weight on top of him. And he realized how lucky they had been, to be trapped so near to the edge of it. The rescuers would never have reached them without proper equipment if they had needed to lift the upper floors away.

The sun was still shining, though now it

was low in the sky. Ben could not believe it was still the same day that he and Carly had set off up the mountain. All around, other rescuers were standing, all of them looking tired and filthy, but all of them happy to see him and Carly crawl out alive. As Carly reached the ground, everyone let out a cheer.

Just beyond the circle of rescuers, Ann Scott, sitting on a lump of broken stone, had Sara in her arms. She held her tight against her shoulder as tears poured silently down her face.

Carly looked around. She was cradling her injured arm, her face one big smile but crying at the same time. She said, 'We made it! We really made it!'

'Yes, but you were very lucky,' her dad said. 'Come on, let's get you down to the first-aid post.'

Ben slowly got up and joined them. Together with his own parents, they limped down the path to the clubhouse.

When they came in sight of the pool area, they saw an ambulance parked outside the reception. Another victim was being loaded inside with the nurse looking on.

'Hey, they got help through!' Carly exclaimed.

'Some,' her dad said. 'The hospital at Verona is receiving casualties. They've already taken Tim.'

They watched as the ambulance started up, its siren beginning to sound as it moved off down the access road.

'And what happened to you?' Carly asked him. 'Tim said you went to the supermarket.'

'We did. We must have slept through the first shock, and there wasn't much to see on this side of town, so we didn't know that anything was wrong until we got to the supermarket. Everybody was talking about it, so we got a report on the car radio.'

'A good thing you can speak Italian,' Ben said.

Mr Scott nodded. 'By then, of course, we were trying to come back here. Then the second shock hit. I pulled the car off the road and we got out and lay flat until it was over. Neither of us was hurt, but it took us ages to get back. The road was damaged, and jammed with traffic, so we had to walk. We got here just as the building collapsed.'

'How did you know we were in there?' Carly asked.

'We didn't know. But we found Tim and

spoke to him, and he said you'd gone in there to look for Sara.'

As he finished speaking they reached the clubhouse, and they sat in the restaurant while John Fletcher went to find out about transport to the hospital. Marian Fletcher brought containers of orange juice and sandwiches for Ben and Carly, while Ann Scott fed juice to Sara with a spoon.

'Food!' said Ben. He'd almost forgotten the taste of food, but now he realized how ravenously hungry he was. He hadn't eaten since dinner with the Scotts, the night before. He'd expected to get back down the mountain for a late breakfast, but not quite as late as this. He couldn't remember anything so delicious as the first swallow of orange juice, washing away all the dust in his mouth. He sank his teeth into a soft roll filled with cheese.

'Make the most of it,' his mum said. 'The water's off, there's no electricity to cook anything, and there won't be any more deliveries for days.'

Ben glanced up at her, but his mouth was full, and it was Carly who asked, 'We're not staying, are we?'

Her father shrugged. 'With Tim in hospital I don't know when we'll be able to leave.'

On the bar, a small portable radio was playing. Graham Scott strolled over to listen more closely.

'Mum,' Ben said, swallowing a mouthful of roll, 'you haven't told me where you and Dad went.'

Marian laughed shakily. 'We went to Venice,' she explained. 'Or at least, when we found your note, your dad said we should go anyway and leave you to sweat it out, so we set off. It was still very early and we got over the Ponte Nuovo before the first shock came. In fact, we felt the shock and heard the bridge go.'

Ben felt chilled. Five minutes later, he thought, and his mum and dad's car could have been one of those lying, twisted, in the river.

'We wanted to come back,' Marian went on, 'but of course we couldn't get across the bridge. We tried driving up one of the mountain roads, to see if we could see you and Carly.'

'I wish you had!' Carly said.

'So then we set off for the next bridge

downriver. Of course, that was miles out of our way. I think we must have missed the worst of the second shock, but we had to leave the car, and it took us ages to get back here on foot.' She sipped her own orange juice. 'They were hauling stones away from where our apartment had been. I saw Ann, and she told me they thought you were under there.' She closed her eyes briefly then opened them again. 'The worst thing was, I'd been feeling so furious with you.'

'Sorry, Mum,' Ben mumbled.

Just then Graham Scott came back from listening to the radio. 'It sounds as if help is on its way,' he reported. 'Towns near by are sending ambulances and rescue equipment. The army are coming in with tents for people whose homes are gone.' He scratched the back of his neck thoughtfully. 'Which doesn't tell us what we should do, of course. We'll need to see the kids into hospital, and take it from there. Luckily we were changing traveller's cheques and so we've got our passports. Have you got yours?'

Marian patted her shoulder bag. 'Everything's in here, thank goodness!'

John Fletcher came into the restaurant and

said, 'There's another ambulance here. Let's get moving.'

Everyone went outside. The noise of an engine was coming from somewhere above them, and Ben flinched, half believing that another shock was about to start; but the sound came from a helicopter that flew low over the resort and vanished in the direction of the town.

The second ambulance drew up beside the pool. Ann Scott went first with Sara, and she stopped to talk to the nurse who had been organizing the make-shift first-aid post.

As Ben approached her, the nurse gave him a brilliant smile. 'You found your family, then?'

'Yes,' Ben said, and he added, 'Thanks for everything.'

The nurse helped Carly into the back of the ambulance where the paramedics were already strapping an unconscious woman on to a stretcher. One of them said something in Italian, and Graham Scott translated.

'He says we're the last batch from here.'

Ben climbed into the ambulance beside Carly. She looked white and exhausted. Her broken arm must have been hurting her a lot, but she still managed a grin. She moved her hand over and clutched his again.

With everyone aboard, the ambulance doors were closed and it moved away, jolting down the uneven road. The siren started.

Ben drew a deep breath. The worst was definitely over. They had come through. And pretty soon, while his dad was still feeling relieved to have him back, he would find time to tell him that he had lost his new camera.

EARTHQUAKES

THE
ESSENTIAL
SURVIVAL
GUIDE

Earthquakes are one of the world's most destructive natural events.
They can happen suddenly, without warning.

If you are caught in a major earthquake, this is what you can expect:

●

Earth movement violent enough to shake you off your feet, make roads buckle, bridges collapse and trains derail

●

Buildings collapsing around you and debris flying everywhere

●

Deadly crevasses that appear suddenly and swallow anything in their path

●

Floods that can sweep you away in seconds

●

Aftershocks that can continue to destroy and kill

NEVER UNDERESTIMATE AN EARTHQUAKE

Warnings

For hundreds of years, top scientists have tried to find a way of accurately predicting earthquakes, but even today this remains impossible.

However, there are some signs to look out for that could mean an earthquake is about to hit:

● Small tremors – just big enough to make small objects fall over.

● Strange animal behaviour – dogs may bark in unison or animals that live underground may come to the surface. (For more on animals and earthquakes see page 19.)

● Weird weather patterns – odd-coloured lights in the sky are often said to mark the beginning of a quake.

● Unusual changes to water levels in natural pools or wells – they can often become lower before a quake.

● Widening cracks and the sudden appearance of holes in the ground.

● Increased activity by local geysers or volcanoes caused by deep rumblings below the earth's crust.

● The ground appears to liquefy – earth can begin to change to moving slime, or bubbling mud.

Shakedown!

If an earthquake strikes, here are some things you could do to protect yourself:

Indoors

Brace yourself against a wall or under a door frame and protect your head with your arms.

Get down on all fours as quickly as possible. You will be more stable and less likely to fall over.

Shelter under a bed, a strong desk or table – try to find something that is anchored to the ground and hold on to it until the shaking stops.

Outdoors

Watch out for flying debris.

Stay away from glass windows. Even if it is reinforced, almost all glass is likely to shatter and could cause serious injury.

Avoid cars. There is a danger that fuel lines could be cut by sharp splinters from bricks or metal debris and the vehicle could easily burst into flames.

Watch the ground – holes could appear very suddenly and they can close up just as quickly!

Move into the middle of an open sports arena or field. It's still the safest place.

4

Aftermath

Ten things you should do after an earthquake:

1

Remain calm and try not to panic. Hysteria will cloud your judgement and may put you at risk.

2

Listen to radio warnings and news bulletins. Help and Rescue centres will be set up in the earthquake zone and you should look for them quickly.

3

Switch off power and water supplies. Be aware of the possibility of leaking gas, which could cause explosions. You should be able to smell it.

4

Stay wary and alert. The danger may not be over. Aftershocks can bring even more devastation, and fire and flooding could be just around the corner.

5

If you are trapped, tap on a pipe or beam. This sound is much more likely to penetrate tons of rubble than a human voice. Rescuers will be able to focus on the noise, which will help them find you.

6

Keep warm. Look for thick clothing and a hot drink, if possible, to help combat any shock. Alternatively, something sweet, like a fizzy drink, will give you a quick boost of energy. Eat food from packets and tins only.

7

Avoid infecting cuts or wounds. Use only clean, bottled water or spit to clean any cuts you may have. Other water sources are likely to become contaminated quickly after an earthquake. Don't drink it.

8

Wear a face mask to protect yourself from particles of dust from collapsed buildings.

9

Watch out for people behaving oddly. Some earthquake victims panic and lose all self control. Avoid looters – they could become violent to protect their stolen goods.

10

Avoid flushing a toilet immediately after a quake. The contents of the system can flood back violently and sewage may escape on to the streets carrying the risk of disease.

Earthquakes
- The Facts

What?

An earthquake occurs when sections of the earth's crust, or 'plates', make a sudden, sharp movement. The points at which these plates meet are known as faults. The way those faults move in relation to each other affects the earth's surface differently.

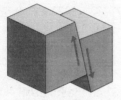

Normal Fault – plates pull apart suddenly

Thrust Fault – plates press together forcing one side over the other

Strike-slip Fault – plates slide against each other horizontally

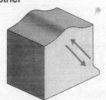

Blind Thrust – plate movement creates hills but doesn't break the earth's surface

Where?

The plate meeting points cover a large area of the Earth. Often the fault lines lie under or close to major cities. Areas commonly affected by quakes include Iran, Romania, Turkey, Italy, Greece, North Africa, California, Mexico, Central and South America, Japan and China. The areas most at risk are Turkey and Japan, where medium-sized quakes hit every year.

EARTHQUAKE HOTSPOTS

When?

Earthquakes can strike at any time. Very few last more than a few seconds. No one really knows why, but when quakes do strike, it is most often in the early morning, usually between the hours of five and seven. As a result, many people are caught asleep in their homes during a quake.

EARTH'S MAJOR PLATES

1 African
2 Arabian
3 Somali
4 Indian
5 Eurasian
6 Philippine
7 North American
8 South American

9 Antarctic
10 Australian
11 Pacific
12 Scotia

13 Caribbean
14 Nazca
15 Cocos
16 Juan de Fuca

8

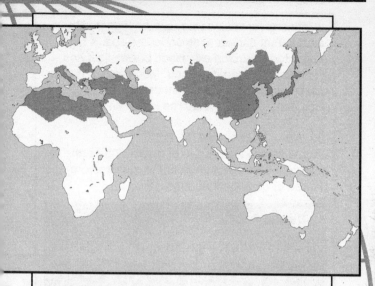

How?

The massive plates that make up the earth's crust are in a constant state of minute movement all the time. When two plates slide into or scrape past each other – like two cars locking together in an accident – they shudder and buckle. Huge pressure and force break the crust of the earth and earthquake tremors spread in waves, closer and closer together.

Effect?

The consequences of an earthquake depend on where it is and how strong the shock is. When it's at full force the ground heaves and moves in waves. Volcanoes and landslides can be set off as a direct result. At sea, huge waves of water, known as tsunami (or tidal waves) can be triggered by shocks from earthquakes under the sea. A big quake can destroy a city. Heat, power, light and water supplies can be cut off. Mountains of debris can fly about; dust clouds, landslides, fire and flood can follow. Lives can be lost in an instant.

Size does Matter!

There are two main ways of measuring earth-quakes: a) the magnitude of the quake and b) the degree of damage it causes.

Time 13.22   13.23   13.24   13.25   13.26

The Richter scale is most commonly used to refer to the magnitude of an earthquake. It was named after the American who invented it – Charles Richter of the California Institute of Technology. A machine called a seismograph records the strength of the tremor by measuring the resulting shock waves. When an earthquake strikes, a machine traces a line, similar to the one shown above. The magnitude of an earthquake is generally represented in numbers from zero to nine.

The intensity of damage caused by an earth-quake could be graded as follows:

A quake so slight that only a very precise seismograph is able to detect it.	**1**
A slight vibration. Few people notice.	**2**
Some movement – enough to wake a sleeping person. Hanging items, like lamps, may swing gently.	**3**
Much more noticeable – objects fall over, buildings shake. Most people will be aware of some movement.	**4**
These tremors begin to be dangerous and to threaten lives. Many old buildings may suffer considerable damage.	**5**
A major quake. Old buildings may collapse, newer ones may be severely damaged. Bricks or masonry will litter the streets.	**6**
Large-scale disaster. Most houses will be destroyed and the area affected will be extensive. Sheltering from danger may well be impossible.	**7**
Catastrophic. These are the big ones. Houses and buildings everywhere collapse. Almost total devastation over a wide area.	**8**

11

Tsunami

'tsu'

'nami'

The word 'tsunami' is Japanese, it translates as 'harbour wave'. Tsunami are huge waves that are triggered by the shock waves of an earthquake under or by the sea. The movement of the seabed sets up a shock-wave ripple – the force of which is converted into energy. The waves will rapidly fan out and mountains of water can run on to the nearest shore at speeds of up to 800 kph (500 mph). The waves are often at their tallest as the huge mass of water hits the shallows.

Aftershocks
Once a major earthquake has struck, further shaking or 'aftershocks' can be expected as the earth resettles. Sometimes, these lesser quakes can be almost as strong as the original earthquake, making rescue efforts difficult. Aftershocks can sometimes still be felt for weeks after the initial quake and should not be underestimated.

Earthquakes
- The Biggies

Some of the biggest earthquakes happen in remote areas where not many people live. Even though those quakes might measure high on the Richter scale, they are not widely reported because few people die. The well-documented record breakers are often the most destructive and deadly quakes that result in huge damage and the largest loss of life. Here are some of the 'biggies':

Place: Mediterranean and the near East **Year:** 1201
Death toll: 1.1 million
Effect: This earthquake hit the Mediterranean and the Near East with such force that it still rates the fifth worst-ever disaster in world history – 1.1 million people were killed.

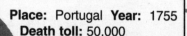

Place: Portugal **Year:** 1755
Death toll: 50,000
Effect: This earthquake hit Lisbon and was felt over an area of a 2.5 million sq km (1 million sq m). During the quake, the sea withdrew from the shore and then

came back at a height of up to 12 m (40 ft) above its normal level. At the time it was noticed that the water of several lakes many miles away – some as far as Switzerland, Sweden, Norway and Loch Ness and Loch Lomond in Scotland – was disrupted. The water in these lakes rose and fell for over an hour!

Place: USA **Year:** 1906
Death toll: 400+
Effect: The earthquake struck San Francisco, California, in six waves from the early morning to 8.45 a.m. on 18 April. Many buildings collapsed. Though few people were killed initially, the damage became huge when fire soon followed and ravaged the shocked city. More than a quarter of a million houses and major buildings were destroyed by either the earthquake or the fire. The richest city in California was devastated. The cost of repairs was to reach a massive $250 million, which is equal to more than $10 billion today. It was the most costly earthquake in US history.

Place: Italy **Year:** 1908
Death toll: 83,000
Effect: During one of the most vicious quakes in history, the entire coastal city of Messina was wiped out and twenty-five surround-

ing towns virtually demolished. In Messina, only one building, owned by a millionaire, was left standing. Fires followed the quake and then, in a biting wind that blew at the ultra-hurricane force speed of 800 kph (500 mph), an 80 m (262 ft) high tsunami ravaged the city. This combination of disasters led to law and order in the area breaking down – only to be restored by Russian and British sailors from the rescue ships offshore. Film of the aftermath of the quake was banned after the scenes it depicted were considered too horrific for public viewing.

Place: Japan
Year: 1923
Death toll: 140,000
Effect: A huge earthquake hit the Japanese capital, Tokyo, and the port of Yokohama on 1 September. Fire swept through the city after the quake and added spectacularly to the devastation. The city arsenal blew up and the gas and electricity systems were wrecked. Convicts ran free. As the fire raged, a tidal wave or tsunami hit the bay and oil on the water was set ablaze. Thousands were trapped between the land fires on one side and the raging torrent of fiery water on the other. More than 700,000 homes were destroyed. The effect of the quake on the landscape was tremendous – the island of Oshima actually moved about 4 m (13 ft).

The ten most deadly earthquakes before 1900

1201 **The Mediterranean and near East**
1.1 million deaths

1556 **24 January – Shaanxi, China**
830,000 deaths

1737 **11 October – Calcutta, India**
300,000 deaths

526 **20 May – Antioch, Syria**
250,000 deaths

1730 **30 December – Hokkaido, Japan**
137,000 deaths

1290 **27 September – Chilil, China**
100,000 deaths

1867 **30 May – Shemaka, Armenia**
80,000 deaths

1268 **Ceilicia, Asia Minor**
60,000 deaths

1755 **1 November – Lisbon, Portugal**
50,000 deaths

1797 **4 February – Quito, Ecuador**
41,000 deaths

The ten most deadly earthquakes of the 20th century

1976	**28 July – Tangshan, China** 650,000 deaths	

1976   **28 July – Tangshan, China**
650,000 deaths

1927   **22 May – Nan Shan, China**
200,000 deaths

1923   **1 September – Yokohama and Tokyo, Japan** 140,000 deaths

1970   **31 May – Northern Peru**
106,000 deaths

1920   **16 December – Gausu, China**
100,000 deaths

1908   **28 December – Messina, Italy**
83,000 deaths

1932   **26 December – Gausu, China**
70,000 deaths

1988   **7 December – North-west Armenia, Turkey** 55,000 deaths

1935   **31 May – Quetta, India**
50,000 deaths

1990   **31 July – North-west Iran**
40,000 deaths

Great Escapes

There have been some incredible stories of miraculous escapes from earthquakes. Since they strike with virtually no warning, the following survivors can count themselves very lucky ...

In the 1963 Skopje earthquake in Yugoslavia a twenty-eight-year-old woman was rescued after being trapped in her hotel room for twenty hours. She had been turned upside down with her bed on top of her and the ceiling only a few centimetres from her face.

After the Columbian earthquake of January 1999, a disabled man was saved after three days trapped underneath tons of rubble. He had been protected by his wheelchair.

After the Al Asham earthquake in Algeria on 10 October 1980, six survivors were found alive after two weeks. They had been in a cafe when the quake struck. They had stayed alive by drinking lemonade.

Lewis Grady, a merchant caught in the quake at Port Royal in Jamaica in 1692, survived because a geyser erupted below him, popping him from a fissure back to solid ground!

After the devastating earthquake in Messina, Italy in 1908, a Welsh sea captain, his first mate Read and a sailor called Smith made an incredible rescue of ten children and several adults from a balcony of the collapsed Trinacria Hotel. Their only equipment was an twenty-centimetre rope to climb up and down.

During the Mexico City earthquake of September 1985, a newborn infant survived in an incubator. The hospital had collapsed around the baby. The infant was found alive under the rubble after fifty-five hours.

In 1940 in Bucharest, a small boy went to bed but woke some time later and walked downstairs because he felt he had to. Moments later an earthquake struck and destroyed his bedroom.

Animal Magic

It now seems that animals may possess some kind of natural warning system to tell them of a coming earthquake. There is evidence that animals behave and act unusually when a quake is about to strike.

Though a big earthquake hit Haiching in China on 4 February 1974, very few people were killed. At least half of the city lay in ruins, but luckily the residents had been evacuated before the quake struck. How did they know they should leave the city? One warning was the strange behaviour of animals. The shy pandas in the zoo stayed out-side, bulls and other animals in the fields moved slowly. Snakes even came out of their hibernation holes, but they were very unlucky – it was winter and they froze to death in the icy air.

In 1939 on the Japanese Oga Peninsula, tuna fish weighing as much as 14 kg (30 lbs) threw themselves on to the beaches. A little later an earthquake struck the coast. There were also stories of octopuses crawling ashore and slithering about as though they were drunk.

During the winter of 1964, Kodiak bears in Alaska were seen leaving their hibernation dens and heading for the hills just before a massive earthquake, measuring 8.4 on the Richter scale, struck the area on Good Friday.

In 1976, dogs began barking loudly in the city of Friuli, north east Italy. Cattle bellowed, cats fled to the country, sheep and deer came down from the mountain tops and caged birds attempted to break free – again, just before an earthquake struck the region.

In 1895, before an earthquake hit Talcahuano, Chile, all the dogs in the town were reported to have left. It seems the dogs were able to feel the slightest movement in the ground, especially through their feet. It is believed they sensed the high-frequency noises made by the rocks far below grinding together, which were out of the human range of hearing.